FJORGYN: A REBEL RISES

RJ CASTIGLIONE

CONTENTS

1

Character name: Creighton Dian-Cecht
Race: Trisian
Age: 27
Class: Druid
Talent: Healer
Level 117 (28,482,031 XP to next level)
Health: 4404 (1512)
Mana: 7533 (1726)
Stamina: 2704 (1260)
Armor: 1,246 (14.4% damage reduction) – 22% damage mitigation
    with skills
Strength: 16
Intelligence: 47
Wisdom: 50
Constitution: 30
Agility: 10
Luck: 14
Alignment: Lawful good (+14)
Racial Traits: None

Profession: Grandmaster Herbalist
Company: Green Shroud Company

"Enthralling" was the only way to explain Fjorgyn Online. While it was an MMORPG, calling it a mere game was an injustice akin to calling PacMan the new pinnacle of gaming design. Fjorgyn was the first of her kind—a completely immersive MMORPG designed to run exclusively through affordable virtual reality. One had to adorn an unflattering outfit equipped with sensory diodes and slip on a comfortable augmentation headset, grab a chair and wake up in the game.

My character was Creighton Dian-Cecht, first of his name—a level 117 Trisian (human) druid capable of massive amounts of healing. I was a proud citizen of Skos, a decent sized nation of all great races. I didn't start that way. I started like many other players, painstakingly fighting my way to the top in both power and profession.

Unlike previous MMORPG's, this game was an experience in immersion. A player could remain at level 1 forever picking flowers in a garden in the village they woke up in, content with ten base points in all stats (aside from luck), adjusted depending on race. Some players dedicated themselves only to professions, becoming merchants, crafters, enchanters, or herbalists. Others still ventured into the wilds as explorers, many never being heard from again.

A player could choose from many races, most torn out of the pages of standard fantasy lore. There were many non-playable races as well. They served as fodder for those seeking power, wealth, or glory.

A player would wake up in any nation, any faction, or any race-appropriate, peaceful location upon starting the game after he or she selected from a litany of playable races and features. The randomness of character creation turned off some casual players who wanted to prance around with friends but attracted a new crowd who wanted the experience of a life away from planet earth, a life where the rules were different, where death was not permanent, and where success was not limited. Instead, opportunities for power and advancement were boundless.

There was no level cap in the game or pre-defined classes. A player was free to choose what he wanted to be.

When I learned I couldn't pre-select my class I was granted a quest to pursue one. It took months of game-time for me to find my first NPC druid. I had to garner reputation with her and convince her to offer me her secrets. I had to dedicate myself wholly to the path of a druid to become one myself. The way of the druid was unique. The rewards upon earning my class — access to unique spells and abilities — were worth the effort.

Beyond winning your class and joining a company, the options were limitless. Given enough time, a player could become a god. The game would adapt and grow to accommodate newfound realms, locations, races, and abilities.

That was the promise anyhow, one that might hardly be achievable in the gamer's lifetime even when taking into account the game makers ability to compress time: pumping the content directly into your cerebral cortex at 400% compression. One hour in the game was fifteen minutes in real life. How would it be fun if one hour of gameplay felt like one hour of gameplay? You could hardly get to a dungeon before people had to sign off.

In real life, I was Michael Semione. In the game, I was the leader of the Green Shroud Company, a tight-knit group of wealthy adventurers. We raided dungeons, organized national events, aided in wars against other factions, and made a healthy profit in training others in abilities while selling crafted goods that no casual player could dream of ever finding on their own. The best part of it all? It paid, too. Selling gold for cash is not only allowed but encouraged. Since the game launched, it became roughly 3% of the nation's GDP.

Despite ample profits from Fjorgyn, I still worked a job every day. It just so happened that I transformed into a grand adventurer at night.

"Creighton! What are you doing?" A fireball splashed at my feet, setting me on fire.

"Ow! Ow! Ow!" The fire licked my skin, causing a debuff. I could see my health ticking away in the corner of my eye, 100hp per second for thirty seconds. Pain in the game was real. The amount of pain that could be felt was also capped. Being stabbed in the chest felt like a bee sting. Getting set on fire felt like walking on hot sand.

"Sorry, Sponge!" I yelled across the cavern while casting a rejuvenation spell on myself followed by channeling Heal (rank 147) on my compatriot. I continued to sling healing spells left and right, pretending I didn't almost die in a fire. The rest of my war party continued fighting the enchanted golem elite boss we stumbled upon while exploring a dwarven ruin. The boss was level 125. As an elite boss, however, he hit ten times as hard, had ten times more health and mana and most definitely ten times more valuable loot once we killed him, at least compared to his non-elite counterparts. There was no reason this boss should have been here. He was definitely a random spawn.

"Get your head in the game! I had 5% health left, and I am almost level 110. I don't want to have to start the level over!" Sponge was always the angry and demanding one of the group. We tolerated him because, like his name, he was the best damage sponge around: A level 109 warrior capable of pulling some mad aggro and keeping the big, bad bosses from having us for dinner. The tricks he could pull contradicted his level.

"Did I ever tell you that I hate golems?" I asked the group. "Fucking health buff!"

The team continued to sling spells and stab away. Not that it mattered much. The thing was made of rock. It resisted everything. What it didn't resist, it healed naturally causing its mana pool to reduce. The only thing that mattered was to fight it until it ran out of mana and fell apart.

With the party now healed up, I analyzed the boss and saw that he had 5% of his mana left. Of his 300,000 mana pool to my 7.5k, there was no way any single player could handle him. Nor was there any reason to bring in a full raid. The ten of us present were enough to bring him down although hardly with relative ease. I was growing weary, and my mana pool was almost depleted. This boss sure had a way to spread out the hurt, and my other healer wasn't pulling her weight on her assigned targets, but after fifteen minutes the boss was finally beaten, crumbling to a pile of rock.

"Woot!" Selena shouted from across the room. I glared at the level 100 gnome priest who managed to survive the fight. Analyzing her, I noticed she had 70% of her MP remaining.

"Thanks for the help, Selena," I mumbled while eyeballing my nearly-depleted mana pool. I had wasted two expensive mana potions while she ran around in circles casting renew on everyone. We had to take her, though. She was the only other healer around who was eligible given her officer rank in the company, a status reserved for those who were Grandmasters of their appropriate profession and in good standing with the company council.

"Chief, come look at this!" That was me: Chief, the leader of the Green Shroud Company.

The group of us crowded around the remains of the golem while Sponge was sifting through the loot. At the center of the pile of rocks rested what many would call a "company killer" – a piece of loot so valuable that fighting for the right to possess it could rip a company apart. It wasn't the power of it. Sure, the soulstone boosted one's attributes by 22 points over the course of 10 levels. The strength was in the removal of consequence. A player could die over and over and over again, never losing all progress earned in that particular level or incurring a negative hit to experience needed to level up.

"Holy shit."

Soulstone of Divine Advancement:

The consumer of this soul stone will receive a one-time +2 increase to all attributes, a +10 increase to all skills, and one additional attribute point per level for your next twenty levels.

Also, the consumer will be granted a divine boon from Balama, the goddess of health and prosperity: perpetual freedom from any and all death penalties.

"Holy shit," I said again under my breath as I picked up the gem. "How can this possibly be in the –"

Before I finished my sentence, the cave shook violently, and a bright flash blinded me. A powerful electrical current encompassed my body.

My brain felt as though it was amplified, like I was plugged into the game five times over.

My vision faded and I dropped the gem only to hear it shatter on the stone floor below. My sight grew blurry, my company members began to pull away, and the world went dark. The last thing I remembered was a loud crack and a jolt of pain at the back of my head.

2
_____

I opened my eyes to a spinning world and a pounding head, like drum beats at the orchestra. When my vision began to clear, I realized that I was laying flat on my back looking up at an opening in a cave. The brightness of the sunlight nearly blinded me again. I snapped my eyes shut in defense. While I slowly opened them to adjust to the newfound light, I felt sharp rocks pressing into my back.

"How did I get out here? This isn't a respawn point." And then I remembered the dwarven ruins, the golem, and the soulstone, the electricity and the blinding light. I winced after recalling the shattering soulstone.

"About time you woke up! I almost thought something went wrong."

I looked around me searching for the mysterious, tiny voice but couldn't find its owner. When my eyes finally adjusted, I saw a crow perched on a boulder next to me. Only crows didn't talk.

Ignoring the creature, I continued to survey my surroundings.

"Hey, birthday boy! Over here!"

My gaze shot back to the bird, now the obvious source of the voice. Birthday boy? As I helped myself up, I realized I was stark naked. I fell to the ground again as I cupped my goods with both hands. I was now flat on my back with my feet planted in the dirt, knees in the air—the perfect perch for the crow to take advantage of. And take advantage he did. With a gentle grace, he glided from the boulder and propped himself on my knee looking down at me, his pointy beak agape. His nails dug into my skin.

Once the embarrassment passed — it was a game after all, and this was obviously an NPC — I relaxed and sat up, looking the crow square in the eyes, unsure of how it was speaking. "What happened?"

"You died." The bird didn't speak so much as project thoughts into my head.

"I know I died. I felt it. It fucking hurt. Why did I respawn here? Why not at the entrance to the ruins?"

The animal looked befuddled.

"There were no ruins, Michael. You died. Really. Hardcore. Epic."

He had used my real name. That wasn't supposed to happen. Perplexed by his response, I continued to examine my surroundings. I wasn't going to get a straight answer from this creature. Crows were notorious tricksters in Fjorgyn. Pushing it off my knee, I stood up to gain a better view of my surroundings.

Map.

A sprawling map opened in front of me, curving around me in a half circle. I saw the cave that I occupied. It was in the middle of a forest. The description only stated "Finlyon Grotto."

I didn't recognize the name. As I zoomed out it was the only discovered location populated on my map — the standard view for any level 1 upon logging into the game. My heart began to race.

Character Sheet

The map was replaced by a similar interface showing my character and my gear, or lack thereof.

Character name: ???
Race: ???

Age: 27
Class: Undefined
Talent: Undefined
Level 1 (83xp to next level)
Health: 100
Mana: 100
Stamina: 100
Strength: 10
Intelligence: 10
Wisdom: 10
Constitution: 10
Agility: 10
Luck: 0
Alignment: Undefined
Racial Traits: None
Profession: Undefined
Company: Undefined

I panicked even more. This had to be the bug to beat all bugs. As I scrolled to the skills page, it was empty. I scrolled to the professions page. Also empty. Disposition page, achievements page, company page, guilds page, professions page all as blank as a piece of printer paper.

Inventory

A single 20-slot bag popped up. Five pieces of stale bread and 5 canteens of dirty water.

Closing my inventory, I felt my body. All vital pieces were in place, but there was something else. My hair was short. My nose was crooked. My body was soft. I was me. Not my character. I was myself. I uncupped my hands. "I have a penis!"

Well. I, of course, had a penis. But characters in the game didn't have junk. Just censored spaces where genitals would be. I was in the game. I shouldn't have had a penis.

"I'm... happy for you," the bird said.

I stumbled backward at the realization and slammed into the wall of the grotto, the rough stone scratching my bare ass. I slid down to the ground like I was over encumbered, the surface cutting into my skin. I landed on a sharp rock and rolled to the side in considerable pain.

-2 HP flashed in the corner of my eye bringing me down to 98 health. Five seconds later, I gained a missing health point and felt the pain begin to fade away as the wound starting to heal.

I felt a sharp jab on my forehead and saw a pebble hit the ground between my legs. The bird was obviously frustrated with me and had flown a circle over me to drop the stone from high in the air.

"I told you. You died. Not your character, Michael. You. While you were in the game, a storm rolled in. Your house was struck by lightning twice in a row. The feedback fried your entire body like a mosquito in a bug zapper. And because of your unique appreciation for this realm, the powers that be decided to reincarnate you here."

Menu.

Nothing happened. Usually, game settings and the ability to log out would appear.

Another stone hit me in the face - my nose this time.

"Beef Jerky! That's not going to work here. And that is the last time I'm going to explain it. Welcome to Fjorgyn."

I felt sick, like I was going to vomit. So I did. I vomited bile and gastric fluids on the ground like a champ, but I quickly stopped after having nothing left to purge. Of course. I was just born and had nothing in my stomach.

The bird flew away flapping its wings in disgust, perching back on his original boulder.

"I'm Vindur, by the way. Thanks for asking. I was appointed to be your guide and companion as long as I decide you need me."

"Vindur, happy to meet you." I swallowed in an attempt to get the taste of vomit out of my mouth.

The crow greeted me with a mocking bow, raising and folding its wing in an empty gesture of pleasure.

"I need a minute," I said to the bird. In truth, I needed more than a minute. I sat down on the cavern floor to take in my surroundings. I was about twenty feet down in a sinkhole. Tension overwhelmed me at the thought of climbing out of there with no clothes or armor. I strained to hear any noise from above. I shouted for help. Aside from the wind and animals of the forest, there was no response.

The large boulder to my left seemed to be Vindur's favorite perch. He pecked at a pile of pebbles to pass the time. Next to him was a white candle. Beside the candle, a large book rested with its cover open. The pages were all blank. There was a brown satchel at my feet — my inventory bag.

A miasma of grief hung over me, like the large roots pouring in from the opening above. I died. Right this minute, my corpse was left undiscovered in my apartment. How long until someone finds my body? How long before my mother and father decide to call the police? I only talked with them once a week. It was Friday night on Earth. No one would miss me until Monday morning. All of the questions I had poured into my mind. I dealt with the confusion and grief by wrapping my hands around my head and resting my elbows on my knees. Tears finally came. And Vindur waited patiently by my side. The bird was kind enough to let me process what had happened to me.

Twenty minutes passed. I cried, I vomited some more, and I cried again. When I thought I was done, I turned to the bird to seek more guidance. I was a blank slate. I needed to know what to do.

"Ready now?"

I nodded at him, swallowing back tears.

"Alright. First order of business. You're you. And that's a problem. We can't have you walking around in your all-together like that. Plus, you look like a flesh-colored, furry pin-cushion. How about you select a race? If you need to review them, they'll be in your journal here." The crow pecked at the book, leaving a dent in one of the pages.

A giant gong sounded, and my interface exploded in front of me – the character creation screen. I didn't have an option in this matter. I tried to close it in vain. It occupied my entire field of vision.

This was the standard creation screen: Race, gender, and customizations. When my breathing finally slowed, I looked through my options:

Trisi: *Completely human in appearance, this is the most common race in Fjorygn. Trisians tend to congregate in and around large cities and are great merchants and diplomats. They have created vast empires. They are average in height and have no special racial abilities. They can excel at magic or fighting and are as versatile as they come. Trisians seem uniquely blessed and are treated with fairness by all the gods. As such, they gain a passive 5% boost to luck and a 5% increase to mercantile and diplomatic skills.*

Mountain Dwarves: *They are stout and muscular with strong backs and arms, but short legs. Mountain Dwarves are tribal and often spend time occupied by infighting between various clans. They are not concerned with the happenings of other races and have a distrust for non-dwarves. They excel at melee fighting, serve as excellent tanks, and are awarded a passive racial skill of night vision – capable of seeing in the dark. They are also excellent craftsmen and enchanters. While mountain dwarves can use magic, they have little affinity. Mountain Dwarves experience the following racial adjustments: +5% strength, +5% boost to leveling all crafting professions (minus herbalism), -5% to stalking, -10% to wisdom, -10% to intelligence. They also enjoy +5% boost to health and stamina regeneration.*

Hill Dwarves: *Like their cousins, the mountain dwarves, they are stout and muscular. They excel in both melee fighting and hunting. While they do establish clans, Hill Dwarves have formed many small kingdoms and inter-clan governments. They are more trusting of non-dwarven races. They have abandoned underground life long ago and have lost the ability to use night vision. Due to their closer proximity to lunar and solar gods, they have regained partial use of magic. As such, they experience the following racial adjustments: +5% strength, +5% boost to leveling all crafting professions, -5% to wisdom, -5% to intelligence. They also enjoy +5% boost to health and stamina regeneration.*

Nisse: *Similar in appearance to gnomes, Nisse are smaller and more slender than dwarves. They are often mistaken for Trisian children. Nisseans live in areas where mountains meet forest and build incredibly advanced settlements and technologies. No Nissean city* becomes too large. When one approaches ten-thousand, a decision is made to create a colony at another location. This results in the formation of clustered kingdoms with a central protectorate. While they can become successful rogues, they have no love of melee combat. Instead, they prefer to be on the fringes of battle and make for avid hunters, spellcasters, and healers. Their affinity for magic also makes them excellent enchanters and herbalists. -15% to strength, +5% boost to enchanting and herbalism, +5% boost to intelligence and wisdom, +5% boost to agility, and +5% boost to mana regeneration.

Elves: *Shorter than Trisians, elves have slender bodies and ears that form a point, often said to aid in hearing beyond the physical realm. They exist in small clans and, though allied, they seldom interact. They adopt both the physical appearance and spell affinity towards the elements they are surrounded by. Due to their size, they have no affinity for melee combat and prefer ranged arts, often exchanging knowledge and skill with the Nisseans. Due to their spiritual attunement and millennia living in forests, their magical gifts are greatly amplified. They also make great enchanters, crafters, and herbalists. They experience -10% to strength, -5% to Constitution, +10% to intelligence and wisdom, and +5% to non-metal crafting, and +5% to herbalism and enchanting. Because of their connection to nature and the divine, they also enjoy +5% to healing arts and +5% to mana regeneration.*

Lizardfolk: *Little is known about Lizardfolk. They are a reptilian species that have no little connection with other humanoid races. They live in swamps and bogs around Fjorygn, never in settlements larger than few dozen. They are partially covered in scales, and their pupils are diamond shaped. They can blend in with their environment due to their existing racial skill, Chameleon. They make great rogues and hunters. They also have an affinity for plant and animal life and make great herbalists. They are able to breathe underwater. +5% to agility, +5% to stalking, +5% to herbalism, +5% to constitution, -5% to intelligence and wisdom. -5% to diplomacy and mercantile skills.*

Catkin: *These people exist in solitary packs all over Fjorygn. They* *have no government structure and have the ability to take on the different appearance of cats. They can also appear Trisian, but the illusion is weak. Sometimes, they even become cats entirely and are able to pass for house pets to the untrained eye. They have a little magical affinity but are skilled thieves and hunters. They are also considered lucky and possess strength beyond their size. They experience +5% to strength, -10% to wisdom and intelligence, +5% to constitution, +5% to luck.*

Giants: *Giants are a clan-based group like dwarves. They look like Trisians, but are much taller and stronger. They have a little magical affinity and find crafting to be difficult because of their large hands and fingers. They make up for this in strength and diplomacy. They are naturally docile and slow to war. As a result, giants are welcome among most races, save Lizardfolk and Catkin who have a natural distrust for them. Giants experience +15% to strength and constitution, -15% to wisdom and intelligence, +20% to mercantile and diplomacy skills, and +15% to health and stamina regeneration.*

My head was spinning with the options and potential. When I first started playing, I chose Trisian because of the deluge of information. I could have always deleted and started a new character. I poured over each option for an hour and then I remembered Vindur.

"What do you think?"

The crow was flying circles above me in boredom. He landed on my shoulder and stretched his tiny talons into my skin. I flinched and tried to pull back but it truthfully didn't hurt that much. "When you played, you enjoyed herbalism and healing. Is that what you want to do?"

I shrugged enough to cause him to lose balance. He compensated by thrashing his wings, smacking one into my face. "I don't know. You're suggesting an elf. What's this adoption of physical appearance and skills all about?"

Vindur explained all about the types of elves — a new mechanic of Fjorygn that didn't exist when I played it as a game. Despite being one race – and the oldest race in Fjorygn at that – they could adapt. Forest elves had fair and tan skin. They could move between trees with ease and could blend in with the forest. They could draw from the magic of forests for healing. The strongest among them could even control the trees themselves. In open country, they were weaker. Mountain Elves had a gray tint to their skin and were excellent climbers. They could command the elements of earth with ferocity and could see underground – but not in darkness at night. I found that peculiar. Darkness was darkness, right? Water elves, called that because of settlements near the ocean, could control water and worshiped Trisian gods of water. They commanded divine magic and could push away or freeze their enemies in their tracks. They were fantastic swimmers and could breathe underwater for extended periods of time. They could even summon storms. When elves were away from their homes for too long, they could adapt new powers, lose their original powers, or both. They could hasten their transformation by meditating in their new environment.

When Vindur explained the adjustment of skills, my mind was made up. Trisians were great and all, but too common. They were "jack of all, master of none." Elves were adaptable, and I wanted to be too. I also did not want to be an unusual race, so big that I could only sex-up giants or so weak in magic that I couldn't heal.

I quickly selected the elven race and adjusted my appearance appropriately. I made myself tall for an elf – still a good foot shorter than my current height. I shortened and straightened my nose. I selected a shoulder-length, brownish-red hairstyle that could be tucked behind my ears. I made my ear points shorter as well. "Sometimes," I thought to myself, "I will need to hide the fact that I'm an elf". I selected what I felt to be the right balance of weight and muscle, making myself lean and muscular, but not "I piss steroids" strong. I left the rest of my face alone but made my eyes a striking gray color. I'd always wanted gray eyes. I was tired of having brown.

When I had accepted my choices, I waited with trepidation for something to happen. Nothing changed. Until it did. My arms shot out from my side while a green light washed over my body. The bulk of my body hair didn't just vanish. It was ripped out, like receiving a full body wax all at once. My screams might have projected for miles.

Notifications in the corner of my eye showed my HP shrinking, then growing, then shrinking, then growing—continuously replenished by the healing spell that surrounded me.

I could feel my spine and my bones all compress. I could hear my hair growing. My ears felt like they would be ripped off my body. My nose crunched as its usual slant was broken, corrected, and healed again. When I thought it was all over, an inferno shot out of my eyes. If I didn't know any better, I could have thought they would boil and drain out. When it was complete, I opened them as best I could, but they were brimming with tears. I had collapsed into a ball on the cavern floor. The pain had subsided, leaving me gasping for air while my eyes fluttered like a spastic butterfly. When I regained some sense of myself, my character screen was all I saw in front of me, shaped like a thin, translucent monitor in my field of vision. I gawked at my appearance. I was not myself anymore. And I still was.

Congratulations! You have selected your race: Elf. Because of your selection in a forest, you have adopted the characteristics of a forest elf and now feel more at home when surrounded by trees.

Closing the character screen, I looked down quickly and felt myself. I was still intact. "I have a penis," I yelled for the second time that night. I lifted my shaft up and gripped underneath. "And balls! And abs! I have abs!" I shook my hands through my hair. "And feel that hair!"

My standard crew cut and pronounced widow's peak were gone. I felt like the Doctor after a new regeneration, only less confused.

When the excitement of possessing my same genitalia wore off, another rock struck me on my new nose. "Now that you have reestablished your blossoming manhood, how about you get going? You seem as though you may be a bit cold." Vindur pointed his wing at my junk. It was retreating from the cold. "And a bit thirsty, and hungry for something more substantial than stale bread." He settled again on the boulder in the middle of the cave.

"Why don't you go find yourself a shirt, some pants, some food, and a weapon while you're at it. You should know the drill. Oh! Get some clean water, too!"

He flew up to the entrance to the cave, landing on a tree root that circled the lip.

"And before I forget, check out your skills page again. The powers above aren't entirely heartless. They wanted to make your experience here a little easier."

DING!

The familiar sound of a character action brought me comfort, making me briefly forget that I was level 1. And naked. And dead. I brought up my character interface again.

Secret name: Slanaitheoir (savior)
Character name: ???
Race: Forest Elf
Age: 27
Class: Undefined
Talent: Undefined
Level 1 (0%, 83xp to next level)
Health: 100
Mana: 103
Stamina: 100
Fatigue: 0%
Armor: -10 (you're naked, jackass)
Strength: 10
Intelligence: 13
Wisdom: 13
Constitution: 10
Agility: 12
Luck: 5
Alignment: Chaotic Good (+1)
Racial Traits: +5% to herbalism, +5% to all non-metal crafting, +5%
    to nature-based healing and damage spells, +5% to mana
    regeneration
Profession: Undefined
Company: Undefined

Modifiers: Forest Elf (+10% movement in the forest)

Skills:

Blessing of Belama (hidden skill, passive): Because of your innate understanding of multiple worlds, your true name is Slanaitheoir – a savior. You will receive more experience from killing creatures and completing quests. You have been granted +2 to all attributes (before racial modifiers). You will also receive two attribute points per level instead of one. You are exempt from all penalties from death. You will not age. You will heal and level faster than others in this world.

Curse of Mannana (hidden skill, passive): Your age will advance at a rate of one year every five years. You will only receive two attribute points per level up to level 20 and then return to one attribute point per level. You may only resurrect at a single, predefined location. The time between death and resurrection will be one week. This position can be changed once per week. You are required to eat, drink, sleep, and void yourself like any other living thing. Failure to do so will result in an increase in your fatigue. Becoming fatigued has consequences! You may only tell allies that you are from another world. "I am Mannana, the Supreme god of death. I am stronger than Belama, and my curse overrides her blessing. I don't know why she is blessing a level 1 elf. I will find out."

By the time I finished reading and closed my character screen, my mouth was agape.

"Stop drooling and get moving, noob!" Vindur obviously had an attitude problem that I hoped I would be able to correct. I was stuck with him for as long as he thought he was necessary. Before I had a chance to leave, another prompt appeared on its own.

You have received a quest! "Shake that moneymaker!"
Vindur has instructed you to find two servings of fresh food, two servings of clean water, clothing, and a weapon. This quest is non-optional.

Reward: Unknown
Bonus: Provide two meals consisting of more than two separate
ingredients. The better the meal, the higher the potential bonus.

I thought this was going to be easy enough, but I recalled my first time logging into Fjorgyn. I started out in a small elven village with clothing, a weapon, and multiple NPC's already procedurally generated with quests to offer. I even had a small amount of coin to get me started. I fostered that small village with other allies I found along the way into a thriving city with my company at the seat of power.

～

Climbing out of the safety of the grotto for the first time was daunting, although I was pleased to find an easy egress. Not only was I stark naked. I was also unarmed. This was a foreign experience for me. I was a gamer. I didn't find myself slogging through the woods in real life, especially naked. Now every thorn pierced my soles. Every branch scratched my body. And every little bug seemed to want me for its afternoon snack. Walking itself wasn't easy. It took me almost an hour to get used to my new body. My stride was shorter. My arms were shorter. I fell a few times, only to eat dirt because I failed to catch myself.

Still, one must do what he must to survive. I continued further away from the cave, crouching and creeping through the trees like a sloth on a hot day. And it was a hot day. Sweat was steaming off me from the heat, leaving wisps of vapor in my wake. As I began to walk further and further, I started surveying the forest floor for any sign of life. It felt like hours had passed before I finally found something to go on, a single scrap of fabric that appeared to have snagged on a branch. The moment I touched the fabric, a notification appeared in front of me.

Congratulations! You have discovered a new skill! Tracking. Your
perseverance in searching the wilds for signs of life has yielded

promising results. Continue to utilize this skill to advance in rank.
Current rank: 1.

When I first started playing, I was overjoyed with discovering my first skill. It wasn't particularly useful and turned out to be my weakest skill at later levels. This time felt different, however. I didn't have the insight and abilities of other players to leverage. I was the only player. The rest? NPC's. In the game, they existed to further my power. I can't say that I ever spent more than a few minutes with any NPC at a time. There was never need.

As I pressed forward, I continued to look for new signs. I saw more broken twigs, but no footprints or other signs of life. If they were there, I wasn't high enough in skill to be able to see them. I had a hunch, though. I continued to follow them for another ten minutes until I saw a temporary structure. I would have almost walked by it if I hadn't turned my head.

Congratulations! You have found 'Abandoned Lean-to.' +10xp

I blinked away the notification and looked around the settlement. It looked abandoned for quite some time. Moss caked the fire pit. Inside the shelter, there was a single pile of moldy leaves, a temporary bed. It looked like the makings of a small lean-to most likely used by a hunter. Behind the bedding, a discarded pouch rested on the ground. I opened the contents of the sack:

Rusty iron dagger with sheath. Quality: Poor. Class: Common
    Weapon: 3-5 DPS. Can be broken by stronger weapons.
Flint and Steel: Can be used to start a fire. Quality: Common
Moldy bread: Once tasty; now worthless.
(2) flasks of fresh water
10 copper

I was more than pleased with this find. I claimed the dagger and tied it to my thigh. Adding the flint and steel to my inventory and taking water and the copper, I saw my own money count in my inventory increase. If this was anything like the game, 100 copper made 1 silver. And 100 silver made 1 gold. Ten copper couldn't buy anything, but it was a start. I closed the pouch and continued to look around, mumbling to myself.

"If I'm going to be successful here, I have to begin thinking outside the box." Eyeing the pouch, I entertained tying it around my 'El Capitan,' but didn't think Vindur would count that as pants. I dumped the moldy bread out and added it to my bag. I noticed then that branches and leaves didn't make the shelter. It was a bit more sophisticated. The inside roof of the tent was fabric, and the support beams were connected by a single cord of rope. Claiming both, I sat my bare ass down to examine the fabric. It was covered in sap and guano and smelled like a dirty armpit. I put on my best MacGyver hat, knowing that it could be repurposed.

I unsheathed my dagger and cut two diagonal lines in the center of the fabric large enough for my head. I then cut four slits two-thirds of the way between the center and the corners of the square cloth and fed the rope through them. Pulling it over my head, I secured the waist by tying a tight knot in the cord. Using my dagger to cut off the ends left two pieces of rope for me to slide into my inventory.

You have created (1) Improvised Cloth Tunic. Quality: Poor. Class:
   Junk. Armor: Light(1). Can be destroyed by weapons. +20xp
Congratulations! You have discovered a new skill! Tailoring.
Your ingenuity resulted in your making a garment you can almost be
   proud of! Continue to utilize this skill to advance in rank and
   create better items. Current rank: 1.

"Three down and two to go," I said to myself. At this point, I needed some food. More importantly, I needed some pants. As much as I loved my dangling bits hanging out, I wasn't sure Vindur appreciated it as much, although it was hard to tell with sentient, communicative birds. At least the tunic covered me. It meant fewer bug bites and scratches.

The abandoned camp treated me well, but now it was time to go. Finding an easier path, I began walking uphill for twenty minutes. The way grew wider and contained more bedrock. My feet thanked me for the relief from thorns and sharp rocks.

Walking up the hillside was tedious and slow. No matter how hard I tried, I could not crouch while setting a fast pace.

Congratulations! You have discovered a new skill! Stalking.
Your dedication to self-preservation has helped you hide from many an
enemy. You now have the ability to stealth through the world.
Increases fatigue. Increase in rank improves hiding, reduces fatigue
increase, and improves movement speed while walking silently.
Current rank: 1.

With my concerns answered, having never utilized stealth before when I used to play the game, I stood up deciding that the fatigue increase was not worth remaining hidden. And this new fatigue information must have been from Mannana's curse. When I played the game, I only had health, stamina, and mana to manage. Fatigue meant I now suffered from common muscle strain, hunger, thirst, and exhaustion. So far, I'd only heard birds chirping and observed the occasional squirrel. As soon as I stood up, however, I felt a sharp pain in my ankle.

Damage received: 22

Flying around, I saw three giant rats behind me. How did I not see them before?

Ripping the dagger from its sheath, I adopted a fighting stance and analyzed the rats. I was grateful this game function still worked. It provided limited data when analyzing enemies while still proving useful.

Creature: Forest rat
Level: 1
Class: Animal
Health: 7

Creature: Forest rat
Level: 1
Class: Animal
Health: 7

Creature: Giant forest rat
Level: 3
Class: Animal
Health: 17

Favoring my injured leg, I decided to attack the ankle-biter first. The blood dripping from its mouth suggested it had a taste for me, and the ability to inflict critical damage. I had a clumsy grip on my dagger, having never fought with one before. It wasn't a staff, but it would have to do. The rat lunged at me despite my raised weapon, leaping through the air to attack my torso only to be dispatched by my blade. I was pleased but was very sure that most creatures wouldn't only throw themselves on my dagger. It was a weak victory. It did substantially more damage to me than I did to it.

Damage dealt: 8 (crit)
Stamina reduced: -10
You have killed a level 1 Forest Rat. +15xp
Congratulations! You have discovered a new skill! Blades. You are now
an agent of death. Continue to utilize this skill to advance in rank
to increase damage when fighting with blades and reduce stamina
consumption. Current rank: 1.
Congratulations! You have discovered a new skill! Light Armor. You
are proficient at wearing light armor. Wearing light armor reduces
movement speed and reduces damage taken. Improve this skill to
reduce speed penalty and increase damage protection. Current
rank: 1.
Damage received: 14
Damage received: 3
Damage received: 9

"Fuck!" I yell at the top of my lungs as the second rat gnawed on my thigh. These notifications were distracting. Grabbing the rat by the tail, I yanked it off and launched it down the path. It landed hard on its back.

Damage dealt: 6
Stamina reduced: -5
Congratulations! You have discovered a new skill! Grappling. You have learned to fight without the use of weapons. Increase this skill to increase damage when fighting in hand-to-hand combat and reduce stamina consumption. Current rank: 1.

When I was distracted by the notifications, the level 1 rat regained its footing and ran at me. I couldn't help but laugh at the creature. It was injured and scurried slower than a newborn kitten. When it approached, I kicked it in the face and sent it flying into the woods like a furry Frisbee.

Damage dealt: 3
Stamina reduced: -10
You have killed a level 1 Forest Rat. +15xp

Before I could regain my footing from my awesome ninja-kick, the giant rat sped towards me and launched itself into the air. Similar to the first, I held up my dagger in self-defense. The stupid rat impaled itself.

Damage dealt: 17(crit)
Stamina reduced: -10
You have killed a level 3 Giant Forest Rat. +35xp
Congratulations! You have reached level 2! You have 2 attribute points to assign. You have gained 10 health, mana, and stamina. 162xp to next level.

Instead of celebrating my victory, the weight of the rat caused me to stumble backward, tumbling down a hillside in an uncontrollable slide.

Damage received: 5
Damage received: 6
Damage received: 5

My elbow slammed into a sharp rock.

Damage received: 15
Damage received: 5
Damage received: 6
Damage received: 5
Damage received: 5

Finally, my free-fall-from-hell-that-causes-falling-damage adventure ended, and I rolled out of a tree line and into an open field. Severely injured with only a few health points left, the low-health and high fatigue alert flashed in my vision. I blacked out for the second time today.

Secret name: Slanaitheoir (savior)
Character name: ???
Race: Forest Elf
Age: 27
Class: Undefined
Talent: Undefined
Level 2 (162xp to next level)
Health: 110
Mana: 114
Stamina: 110
Fatigue: 0%
Armor: -10 (you're naked, jackass)
Strength: 10
Intelligence: 13
Wisdom: 13

Constitution: 10
Agility: 12
Luck: 5
Alignment: Unknown
Racial Traits: +5% to herbalism, +5% to all non-metal crafting, +5%
to nature-based healing and damage spells, +5% to mana
regeneration
Profession: Undefined
Company: Undefined
Modifiers: Forest Elf (+10% movement in the forest)

Skills:
Novice Blades 1: The ability to deal damage with knives and blades.
Drains stamina. Increase in rank reduces stamina drain and
increases additional damage.
Novice Grappling 1: The ability to deal physical damage through
hand-to-hand combat.
Novice Light Armor 1: Wearing light armor grants a bonus to damage
reduction. Increase in rank improves movement speed and reduces
damage taken.
Novice Stalking 1: The ability to stealth through the world. Increases
fatigue. Increase in rank improves hiding, reduces fatigue increase
and improves movement speed while moving silently.
Novice Tailoring 1: The craft of creating cloth armor and goods.
Novice Tracking 1: The art of finding your way through nature. Useful
for hunting creatures or humanoids alike. Also aids in discovering
new paths.

3

"Michael, wake up! Wake up, Michael!" I felt a sharp beak pecking at my forehead.

"What happened?" I groaned. I was no longer laying on the ground. And it was no longer daytime. Instead, I was in a carriage. No — a cage being drawn by a carriage. And it was well past sunset. I was surrounded by a group of miserable looking people of various ages, races, and genders. There were ten of us in the cage, all low level.

"You tell me," Vindur said, his yellow eyes only inches from mine. There was a slight hint of fear in his voice. Fear and concern. His smooth coat of thick, black feathers was standing on end as though he had been run through a dryer. "One minute I was perched on a branch. The next moment I found myself resting on your beaten, bloody body in this hellish cage. And what are you wearing?"

I looked down at my body. While my wounds were gone and my health was now full, my skin was caked in dry blood, sap, and mud. My tunic was torn to shreds. I barely had any energy. My dagger was gone, and my fatigue was now dangerously high. This caused a silent debuff that reduced my health, stamina, and mana.

I hushed Vindur, worrying that the others in the cage might find it odd that I was talking to an eloquent flying crow.

"Don't 'hush' me! They can't hear me. They can't see me. And they can't see or hear you talking to me. I'm an agent of Balama. I have that power."

"Okay, okay," I said. "I encountered… difficulties. A few hours into the hike, I found a hunter's tent. I stripped it down and made this tunic. Learned to tailor, by the way. So don't laugh at it! When I left the tent, I ran into some forest rats. That's when shit went crazy. When I was fighting them, I was overwhelmed with notifications. They distracted me, but I still beat them, only… I tumbled down a hill in the process and blacked out. I woke up here."

After my brief recap, I couldn't tell if Vindur was going to lash at me again or burst out laughing. He chose sarcasm instead. "Why not just turn off the notifications, soup for brains?" he asked with a pristinely patronizing tone.

"How? I don't have access to the menu."

Now he started cackling. "Just will it. You can control anything in your interface, including notifications and display information on your character screen. You can also will a health bar over your enemies and allies and turn off the damage notifications. You don't need to see the damage you receive. You can already see it in your field of vision at all times." He paused slightly, examining our surroundings further. As he explored the cage, he continued to talk.

"And you can set your interface, so that skill information and fight summaries queue up to review when you're done… or dead." He stopped speaking to perch on the head of a taller-than-anyone humanoid while poking his head out of the top of the cage. "We're in a slaver caravan."

"What?!"

Apparently, my exclamation was not specifically targeted at Vindur, and the rest of the captives were startled. A little girl in the group began to whimper, burying her face in her mother's breasts. Vindur lost his balance and fell to the floor.

"Quiet in there, scum," a guard said while cracking his sword against the bars near my head.

"Vindur, there's no slavery in Skos. At least not of high races."

"Well. This must not be Skos, then. What does your map say?"

I opened my map and shrugged. The game map always revealed what nation you were in and relevant information about particular zones within. This map didn't have those features. It was just updating where I had been. And right now all I saw was a clear, jagged line leading back to Finlyon Grotto, my only known sanctuary.

"Well, fried chicken, you best quietly ask these people here. I'm going to explore a little." Vindur seemed proud of his "fried chicken" joke. I didn't find a joke about my prior death hilarious. Okay. It was a little funny.

"Too soon," I mumbled.

Examining the people in the cage with more care, I could tell that many of them were like me: low-level individuals who were struggling to get by. They were all dirty, but I felt as though they all knew one another. Half were young; half were old. Many were women and children with only three men in the group. One of them appearing to be half-giant. The rest were Nissean, elves, or Trisian. I didn't see any dwarves, lizardfolk, or catkin. Like me, none of them had a company or class. And like me, they all had an aura of desperation about them.

> *Congratulations! You have discovered a new skill! Observation. You have become keenly aware of your surroundings. You can glean useful information from people and the world around you to aid in your understand of your world. Practice this skill, and you will find yourself well on your way towards understanding how the world works. Current rank: 1.*

I quickly dismissed the notification, turning my attention towards a young woman closest to me. In an almost inaudible whisper, I asked her if she knew who our captors were and where in the world we happened to be.

She shot me a surprised expression, looked me up and down, shivered a non-verbal "go away" and turned from me. She must have thought me a wild elf. I certainly looked the part of a crazed lunatic – like Tarzan, only without the loincloth.

"We're in Vros," a Trisian captive whispered. "Heading to the slave markets in Elatha." A second guard beat his pummel against the cage, silencing us all. The man was defiant. Without drawing attention to himself, he passed me a pair of pants and a shirt one of them had in their inventory.

> *Homespun Cotton Trousers. Quality: Good. Class: Common. Armor: Light(2). Can be destroyed by weapons.*
> *Homespun Cotton Shirt. Quality: Good. Class: Common. Armor: Light(2). Can be destroyed by weapons.*

I put on my best smile and slipped the pants and shirt, discarding my blood-soaked rags, but keeping the rope. The clothing was comfortable, the first experience of comfort I have had since my rebirth.

Vindur soon returned and settled on my shoulder, shaking his wing in my ear to announce his arrival. He gestured to my bag without saying anything. I examined my inventory and found a dozen servings of ripe bananas and a dozen of salted cashews.

"How did you get this in there?"

"I can add things I find to your inventory myself. I don't have to be here. I liberated these from the guards."

Thanking Vindur with a profuse smile, I passed the food around in silence, leaving two servings of both for my companion and me. We ate the food and drank the fresh water in my inventory. I was shocked that Vindur was able to stuff down all of it. I could feel my fatigue reducing. When I took the last bite, I received an immediate notification.

> *You have completed the quest: "Shake that moneymaker!"*
> *Reward: +95xp*
> *Bonus reward: +40xp for good quality clothing.*
> *Bonus reward: +30xp for a two-ingredient meal.*
> *Congratulations! You have reached level 3! You have 2 attribute points to assign. 273xp until next level.*
> *Congratulations! You have put your own safety at risk to provide food to a group of hungry and scared people. In doing so, you have stood against the realm's established laws and protocols for the proper actions of slaves. People will recognize this goodness in you*

*and respond appropriately in all future social interaction. Your
actions have rewards. They also have consequences. This
expression of goodness may also vilify those around you who
pursue evil. Your actions may also distance those who wish to
follow the rule of law.*

Without hesitation, I opened my character interface and saw my
four free attribute points instead of the expected two. Thinking back on
level one and mulling over my experiences so far, I realized that my
previous path of magic was not going to be nearly as easy in this mani-
festation of Fjorgyn. I had to get stronger and I needed more health. I
had plenty of time. I could always increase my wisdom and intelligence later. I allocated two points to strength, two points to constitution. When I submitted my changes, I felt new health within me. I was
more vibrant. My muscles felt more capable and sturdy. I was more
flexible and physically fit.

The rest of the captives had finished eating and were all eyeballing
me with looks of surprise and confusion. Whispering among themselves, they questioned how I had managed to level up when locked in
a cage. "What is your name, stranger?" the Trisian man asked me.

I thought about this question for a second. I was no longer
Creighton Dian-Cecht. Creighton died in a game. I briefly imagined the
reaction of my company companions when I shattered the most valuable item we have ever found and dropped dead never to resurrect
again. I can picture the bones of my corpse resting for a few days in
that Dwarven chamber until the game's procedural algorithms cleaned
them up. Will they ever know what happened to me? No one in the
game knew anyone's real name. There was a mental block preventing
players from sharing personal information that persisted even when
one was offline.

I still wanted to be Dian-Cecht, though. The surname had signifi-
cance for me as a reference not only to the Celtic god of healing but to
my personal desire to heal others as my primary function. I also
wanted to be Michael again. I didn't want to forget that part of myself.

"Michael Dian-Cecht," I replied. They all smiled and offered their
greetings, although some were a tad surprised with my unusual name.

I possessed a name of a Trisian and the last name of an elf. But I was completely elf.

A third guard rattled the side of the cage and ordered quiet. Silence and sadness washed over the group like a great thunderstorm meeting a quick end. What was missing now was desperation. It had been replaced by the smallest kernels of gratitude and respite.

Congratulations! You have increased a skill! Observation. Current rank: 2. You are 1% more likely to glean useful information from people and things around you.

Pleased with my character progress for the first time, I took my cue from those around me, rested against the cold iron bars of our cage, falling into a disruptive and shallow sleep. I was going to need my strength to face what was to come, especially if that involved escaping slavery.

Secret name: Slanaitheoir (savior)
Character name: Michael Dian-Cecht
Race: Forest Elf
Age: 27
Class: Undefined
Talent: Undefined
Level 3 (274xp to next level)
Health: 123
Mana: 124
Stamina: 123
Fatigue: 0%
Armor: 4 (.05% damage mitigation) – 1.05% with skills
Strength: 12
Intelligence: 13
Wisdom: 13
Constitution: 12
Agility: 12
Luck: 5
Alignment: Chaotic Good (+1)
Racial Traits: +5% to herbalism, +5% to all non-metal crafting, +5%
    to nature-based healing and damage spells, +5% to mana
    regeneration
Profession: Undefined
Company: Undefined
Modifiers: Forest Elf (+10% movement in the forest

Skills:
Novice Blades 1
Novice Grappling 1
Novice Light Armor 1
Novice Observation 2
Novice Stalking 1
Novice Tailoring 1
Novice Tracking 1

4

"I've heard about these things before, you know: Invaders overwhelming a small village with torches and swords. When I found out about them, I tried to picture the fights in my head. Now I know that I never understood 'real war.' It was the first time I experienced such things, but that didn't stop over half of my village from being slaughtered. This always happened elsewhere. This always happened to other people. To me, those who were attacked and captured by slavers deserved it. That is what they told us. Slaves were deserving for their crimes against the empire – that they sinned against the High Protectorate of Elatha; that they were criminals who were punished by having to earn their freedom again. Then the soldiers came in the night and captured my wife, my children, and any villager who couldn't get away. They killed those who fought back. I learned then that it was all propaganda."

I listened intently to him. The guards had left us alone and we were now free to speak. "Go on," I instructed. I was curious to hear his story.

"We were simple farmers. Hardly one of us ever ventured out far enough from our village to reach level 10. We never caused anyone trouble. We provided enough to sell what we needed to the capital and feed our families for the winter. Moga," he gestured to the level 11 Nissean in the group, "was the most experienced of us - a hunter. The soldiers arrived fast enough where he didn't even have a chance to grab his bow. We ran; my wife and children and I. We moved with the rest of the group as far as we could for as long as we could run. It didn't matter. The slavers caught us on their horses. Once they had our children, the fight was over. There was nothing more we could do. If we struggled, our kids would be orphans."

"But you would have respawned, right?"

The man, now known to me as Cilden Thane, glared at me as though I were speaking another language. He had bright red hair with a beard to match. His hands were strong and dirty from years of working the land. I guessed that he had never held a weapon before. He didn't seem that type. He was innocent. He and his family were truly undeserving of the abuses they have experienced.

"Oh yeah. I forgot to tell you. Others in this land do not respawn like you do. Once they die, they actually die." Vindur was "always" prompt with his necessary information. I pushed him off my shoulder to punish him for his tardiness with important details.

"Sorry, my mistake. What I meant to ask is whether the soldiers really would have killed you in front of your children. They're slavers. They make money by selling slaves… us. They have no profit if they kill every new slave who resists."

Cilden shrugged, expressing complete resignation. "I would not have us be parted." He bounced his little daughter on his lap while his wife, Rose, tended to their son.

It had been five hours since we arrived at the outskirts of Elatha, the capital city of Vros. The guards unloaded us, welded a black leather collar around our necks, and placed us in a caged paddock for the remainder of the night. There were now fifteen of us waiting eagerly to be sold to our future masters. We had joined a group of five individuals who were already in the cage.

I learned through my new friend that Vros was an empire on the opposite side of the planet from Skos. Where Skos was a free-market democracy, Vros was a meritocracy, an oligarchy if one was to be exact, with Elatha as her capital. It was also a nation that favored enforced slavery among the poor and downtrodden. Slavers were known to invade small villages and towns and capture people to meet their quota. Those captured, which now included me, were sold on the open market to members of the aristocracy as personal servants and house slaves. Some were sold to the mines. The prettier women and boys among slaves were sold to whorehouses. Enforced slavery kept the economy moving.

"We can be back at Finlyon in a week," Vindur said. "Just get a guard to kill you."

It was a decent idea. I could best spend my time on leveling and improving my skills. Unless I was going to spend my time hunting forest rats, though, I would have to leave the forest eventually and would most likely find myself back here. And who knows. If I were to antagonize the guards and get them to attack, they might not stop with me. They could decide that our entire group was not worth the hassle and slaughter us all in a matter of minutes. Screw the profit loss. They could choose to sell the children into the worst positions possible.

"No. My nation decided long ago that slavery was an abomination. I'm going to stay here and do all I can to help these people. Plus I'm going to live for another 350 years or so. I don't want to escape through death whenever it is convenient for me, especially when I have to wait a week to resurrect again."

Vindur detested my stubbornness, hopping off my shoulder to explore.

"Death fucking hurts!" I told the crow.

"I'm sorry, Vindur. Am I upsetting you? Is this cage not to your liking? You can always fit between the bars. Go. Find out what you can learn."

Without hesitating, Vindur heeded my command and flew away.

"Cilden, where I come from, slavery is unacceptable. We used to have slaves. My country divided in two: North for abolition and south for separation. Both sides waged a great war that cost hundreds of thousands of lives. The victors decided the question of slavery: never again." I measured my next words carefully. I never imagined myself a hero before. That's why I always liked healing. It let other people be the heroes. Still, these people needed me. I had found potential allies, and I wasn't going to abandon them to slavery. If they needed a hero, I could become one.

"I will see you and your family out of this if it's the last thing I do. I promise."

You have received a quest! "Let my people go!"

You have promised to free yourself and your friends from slavery. Be a savior to your adopted people! Find them a new settlement. You will have six months to accomplish this quest. This quest is not optional.

Reward: Unknown

Bonus: Additional rewards will be given depending on the number of unknown individuals you also free. Additional rewards will be given depending on the quality of the settlement.

The burly man smiled, not sure what to make of my proclamation. In his mind, I could tell that he thought my words were hollow. How could a level 3 elf get him and his family away from Elatha? And how could a man such as myself who was older than him be found at the edges of a forest and still only be level 3?

Despite his apparent disbelief in me, I was brimming with resolve. I would see them through this and would free as many slaves as I could in the process. We would escape to build a new home out of reach of the arm of Elatha.

Congratulations! You have discovered a new skill! Leadership. Your willingness to lead others results in their seeing you as a natural and efficient leader. Increase this skill to improve the loyalty of those who you lead towards accomplishing your goals and fulfilling your purpose. Current rank 1.

"Tell me about Elatha."

Children heard many stories about the dark city. Traders would come to the village, selling goods but giving stories in exchange for food. It was perpetually clouded in night – a darkness inspired by magical barriers maintained by the Wraithheart Company, a group consisting of the most wealthy citizens of the city. The oligarchs of this company, called the "High Protectorate," ruled with an iron fist. One would only earn their respect by becoming rich and powerful like themselves. Their grip on the city's economy made accomplishing that an impossible feat. The city consisted of four rings all divided by extensive systems of canals. There were 500,000 or so residents, two-thousand among them members of the aristocracy. The inner ring was for the ruling members of the Wraiththeart Company and their families. The second ring consisted of aristocrats who were members. The third ring consisted of non-membered, skilled laborers. The outer ring was made up of slums, housing unskilled freemen. On top of the 500,000 residents, there were twenty to thirty thousand slaves.

He spoke of the economy, the people, and the politics. By the time he had finished, an hour had passed, and the barrier he alluded to began to glow, lit up from the outside by the morning sun. Despite the power of the company, even they could not create a complete and perpetual night. They could merely blot out the sun. The barrier was still impressive. I had never heard of or witnessed such a futile exercise in magical power. What was the purpose? This was the capital city. Surely everyone knew where it was. I could understand a protective shield encompassing her circumference. A protective barrier that blocked sunlight was another thing entirely. It was an exercise in blatant suppression.

With the conversation completed, the fifteen of us sat in silence. I finally got my first chance to look at my fellow prisoners in more detail. Cilden was always the most visible, along with his children. The three shared shoulder-length, ginger hair. Cilden and Junta, his young son, both had square faces and broad shoulders. Analyzing Cilden, the man was rank 21 in agriculture and rank 8 in Construction. He was also rank 13 in "Creature of Burden," most likely due to lifting heavy loads all day. His son, despite being only six, had the look of a boy who helped his father in the fields. Both Junta and Neeta, his daughter, had some softer features as well. Their ears stuck out of their hair, though, coming to a faint point – inherited from their mother, an elf like me.

There was Moga, the Nissean hunter. He had scars crossing his face as though a large predator clawed him. He wore a green tunic and leather trousers that contained more patches than pant. I analyzed him. All of his skills were higher than his own level. He was rank 25 in stalking and rank 18 in archery. His light armor skill was also high. Others in the cage, mostly farmers by their appearance, were lower level than Cilden. I spotted a half-giant in the back, a man named Baridorne, but couldn't see much of him through the crowd.

~

"Father, no! I don't need them. Look at them. They're all filthy!"

The silence broke when a squad of soldiers escorted a stout man and his prat of a twenty-something son to our jail. The older man examined us, covering his nose in disgust. He evidently considered us beneath him. And for now, we were.

"Nonsense," he said to his son. "You already disobeyed me by not taking the wife I selected for you. Now that you've decided to run your own household, I'll not see you servant-less. No son of mine is going to wash the dishes like a lowly kitchen bitch. We have a reputation to maintain."

If there weren't bars between us, I would have broken the man's nose. How could anyone justify prospering on the backs of slaves? He continued.

"And this lot will do nicely once you clean them up. They're low level, especially that cockroach of an elf in the corner." He pointed at me. "Honestly. Why do we let them breed so much? You have men to do the heavy lifting, women to cook. You can even fuck them if you want. And look! Children to be your little spies!"

He motioned over to the clerk and informed him that they would take the lot of us for 15,000 gold. My stomach lurched at the cost. 1,000 gold was enough to start a small village. And this man was paying the price for a cluster of slaves to do his son's bidding. The pudgy clerk nodded and jotted down some lines in a small notebook he clutched in his petite hands. Once he gave the older man what appeared to be a series of fifteen scrolls, soldiers rushed into the cage and lined us all up, treating us like the prisoners we were. They threaded a rope through a ring in our collars to bind us all together, tying a knot to the end to prevent us from escaping.

> *Attention: You have been sold into slavery. The knowledge that you are now property owned by someone else weighs down upon your soul. All attribute points reduced by 3 until you secure your freedom. You now have the "mark of the slave," a collar that cannot be removed by ordinary means.*

"Damn. That sucks," I mumbled under my breathe.

We were escorted out of the pen area, and I got my first glimpse of Elatha. I was asleep when we had arrived.

> *Congratulations! You have found 'Elatha.' +40xp*

It took us two hours to walk from the slave pens on the outer ring of the city. Elatha reminded me a fair bit of Beijing, not that I had ever been there. The concentric rings were connected only by crossroads in the shape of an asterisk. This made for a longer trek. We had to walk two miles before we encountered the first road that reached the second ring. We took a right and crossed through from the outer ring to the second ring. The buildings grew in both size and stature. The dirt and huts of the outer ring became wooden houses and stone paths of the third. The second ring consisted of buildings made of off-white masonry and blue cobblestones. At the end of the road, we were required to walk a quarter mile back to the center of the city with a three-story, red wall on our left-hand side. Inside it was the inner ring, a large area containing the most wealthy members of this society. The entire capital seemed more like an underground lair than a prospering metropolis. It was cold and stuffy, absent the warmth of the sun on our skin.

Our new owner wasn't walking, of course. They had tied us to his wagon. It had taken a great deal of convincing and a lash or two before they allowed us to carry the children. Rose, Cilden's wife, was inconsolable and in a silent state of shock once we were purchased. I had to take their daughter for them. This wasn't easy. Neeta was about four years old. She weighed about thirty-five pounds. Her half-elven ears kept twitching whenever they picked up a new sound.

The trek wasn't entirely in vain. I learned a new skill called "Creature of Burden" and increased it to rank 5, reducing my fatigue drain when performing manual labor. And I improved my standing with Neeta to friendly. I learned that disposition of children was very easy to raise. They would trust anyone their parents liked. Even though the girl was only four years old, I didn't mind. I would take any ally I get, even if this ally's particular gift is pinching my cheeks, tugging on my ears, and pulling my hair for amusement.

There were worse things in the world. Like being a level 3 slave. In a city cast in perpetual night. Run by maniacal oligarchs. Who had more combined power than a thousand level 100 grandmaster wizards. I was really going to have to rethink my approach to life.

When I played the game, I exclusively resigned myself to healing and professions. That certainly wasn't going to cut it here.

How I longed for the endless days of summer one finds in Skos. Why couldn't I have been reborn there? While I was at it, why couldn't I have been resurrected on Earth? I wanted my mother. No man ever outgrows the need for his own mother when times gets tough. "Damn it," I mumbled to myself.

5

The group of us were marched through open plazas and by gardens that glowed silver. Because of the appearance of being magically polished, the inner ring was among one of the most beautiful sights I have seen in all of Fjorgyn. The inner city had a miasma of jasmine, one of the most common herbs known, serving as a base ingredient for various useful potions and tonics. It was opulent.

As we were led deep into the district, the scent faded. The gardens no longer sprouted white jasmine flowers but contained many ingredients, some known to me. One garden exclusively included moon grass, a rare and expensive ingredient used in both health and invisibility potions. I made a mental note of its location in my head. If I could somehow gather enough of it along with a few other ingredients that I needed, I could fashion us an exit from Elatha.

I was too lost in thought to realize we had stopped, bumping into the side of the wagon. No one noticed. It appeared we had arrived at our new home and prison, a beautiful four story mansion made from white stone.It had a blue-tiled roof and high walls encompassing the entire estate.

White pillars supported the roof. The massive doors of the house were open, most likely to let in the unexpectedly cold air in the city. In the courtyard in front of the home, a giant fountain sprayed a single stream of water. It filled a central basin, pouring into two lower tiers before emptying into a pool at the bottom. The bottom basin, twenty feet in diameter, also contained a fair number of aquatic herbs that I knew from sight alone.

I finally understood how the elites of this city maintained their grip. They prospered on a monopoly of magic and herbalism.

Standing beside the fountain was a single brazier illuminated by a blue flame. There was a poker sticking out of the flames with a durable leather grip.

"That's not a poker, you know. It's an enchanted brand." I jumped at the sound of a familiar voice.

"Where have you been!?"

The bird settled on my shoulder - his now all-too-familiar and most favorite roost. Neeta's sleeping head occupied my other shoulder.

"Exploring as you commanded. We can talk about this later. First I am going to apologize."

"Apologize? For what?"

The rope tying us together was cut and ripped out of the ring in our neck collars. Now surrounded by guards who had swords at the ready to slice down anyone who attempted escape, our pudgy buyer silently glided to the brazier. For a man of his size, I was amazed that he possessed grace enough to move in silence.

"Welcome. I am Lord Clifford Grey. My son, here, is your new master, Clifford Grey II." There was an echo of disdain in his voice when he said 'the second.' "He is to be obeyed in all things for the duration of your service to our great and noble house. Obey him, and you will be treated with respect. Disobey him, and you will be punished. Severely. When I call your name, please step forward to receive your mark."

"I apologize… for this. I don't think Balama meant for us to follow this path. I failed you in my guidance," Vindur whispered. There was sadness to him I have never heard from him before.

"Cilden Thane, level 7."

Cilden left the line and walked forward to stand in front of his new master. Two guards rushed him, pulled him to his knees and pulled his shirt down his arm to expose his shoulder, ripping the fabric in the process. The younger Clifford turned and walked away, triggering a look of disapproval in his father's eyes. It faded, however, and was replaced with a devilish grin as he picked up the brand from the brazier. "This mark is the sigil of our house. It must be made visible upon request from any freeman of Elatha." Lord Grey chanted a few words under his breath and forcefully pressed the brand into Cilden's shoulder. I could hear the sizzling of Cilden's skin as the brand glowed a bright azure. Blood bubbled as metal melted into his skin like a warm knife through soft butter. Cilden shook in pain, but let out no scream.

He was lifted to his feet and allowed to stumble back into line. Claiming his sleeping daughter from my arms, he whispered to me. "Please don't scream. I do not want to scare my children." His lip was bloody, having bitten into it to suppress his agony. A stream of tears ran down his face leaving only a trail of clean skin behind.

"Michael Dian-Cecht." I repeated the process. When the brand bit into my shoulder, an electric pain filled my entire body.

Damage received: 117

Attention: You have been branded a slave belonging to the house of Grey. The brand is enchanted. Until you escape or earn your freedom, you may not leave the entrapment barrier surrounding Elatha. Any attempt to cross the barrier will result in a health loss double that incurred upon being branded.

Your resurrection point has been fixed to the home of Clifford Grey II. This location cannot be changed until the completion of "Let My People Go!"

The notifications distracted me enough from the pain. I was able to contain everything beyond a quiet whimper. In my current state, I was sure I could be mistaken for an injured dog. With tears welling, I returned to my place in line while the others went through the same process. Clifford Grey didn't spare the children the agony of the mark. Their screams of terror broke my heart.

After the marking ceremony, if one could call that monstrous injustice a ceremony, the fifteen of us were brought to a basement corridor consisting of three bedrooms, a single washing facility, and a small kitchen and lounge. Because of Neeta's persistence, "Uncy Michael" was able to remain with the Thane family. I didn't know when the girl decided to consider me an uncle. Her parents didn't argue with her. She was injured and still on the verge of tears. The remainder of our group chose their rooms, some with family and others with complete strangers.

With doors finally shut, the horrors of our being sold and magically marked faded somewhat. Rose knelt beside her children and examined the mark, a circle with a portrait of an owl within it. Blood had soaked into their shirts. She called for their removal, along with Cilden's and mine, and set the bloodied shirts aside. Part of me was sad to separate from it. The shirt represented the first act of kindness bestowed upon me in Fjorgyn. I quietly hoped it would not be the last.

Then Rose did something amazing. Hovering her hands above her children's arms, a white light emanated from her palms and washed over their skin, soothing the burn and stemming the flow of blood.

"You're a healer," I stated in disbelief. The low-level woman had cast healing touch on her husband. His health slowly replenished while his wound magically stitched itself closed. Sure. The scar remained. It was a magical mark after all.

She explained her skill while repeating the process on me. "Not in so many words. I have a skill in healing like so many of my people. You're an elf. I'm surprised you don't possess some healing ability. Then again, you seem to be an elf who is full of many secrets, like being found nearly dead on the side of the road only to be back to full health a few hours later. You'll have to tell me more about that."

The same white glow washed over my skin and my health had also trickled up to 25% full. "There, Neeta. Uncle Michael is all better." Rose didn't sound happy with the thought of me, a complete stranger, being held in high regard by her daughter.

The girl gave out a gleeful cheer and beckoned for me to play with her. I had to oblige. These people took me in and trusted me with their children. They showed kindness even in the face of insurmountable challenges.

I held one of Neeta's hands above her head as she spun around like a prima ballerina, having completely forgotten her earlier torture.

"Rose." I hesitated to ask the question. "Can you teach me to heal?" I looked at her while the same soft-white glow washed over her arm.

While she expressed a strong desire to teach me, she explained in as few details as possible that her skill was not high enough. To teach me to heal, she had to raise her healing rank to level 30. She was currently level 4. Given the circumstances, she couldn't heal frequently enough to raise it any higher. It had taken her years of scrapes and cuts even to raise it as high as she did. And unless someone was willing to mutilate himself, she wouldn't be able to force the level high enough in a mean-ingful amount of time.

When everyone settled in for the night, I took my leave and went to the washroom. Removing my clothes, I sat on a cold, wooden stool, pouring water over my head and wept. Not from pain, but in grief over my death, the separation from my family, and the newfound horrors of the land I had once thought a second-home. I always knew there were darker and more dangerous nations in Fjorgyn. I had, however, been perfectly content remaining in Skos. There was always plenty to do. The never-ending stream of quests and tasks prevented me from crossing into other nations before.

Washing away the shit and mud and blood and tears was the therapy I needed. Vindur granted me my moment of introspection, himself also overwhelmed by his charge's misfortune.

I wasn't alone in my despair. Another young man, barely twenty, had also taken the opportunity to wash. He sat in the corner, his back turned from me. The points of his ears twitched in response to the cold water he poured over his head. I left him alone as well. Neither of us had any interest in making new friends right now.

A grand plan was born in my head on the night of our forced servi-tude. Over the next week, we cooked, cleaned, did laundry, tended horses, bought trade goods for the master, and received the occasional lashing for taking too long. Never from the master, though. His paid guards weren't as forgiving as him. He talked to each one of us individually to determine what skills we were best at. He was surprised upon meeting me. I was the same level as a four-year-old and had no aptitude for anything.

"Tell me more about yourself," he said. He had brought me into his private study where he had talked to the others in more public settings. "Your fellows know nothing about you. You didn't come from their village. They said the guards found you on the edge of a forest next to the corpse of a giant rat – one that you had apparently killed. Now how does a level 3 elf end up trekking through the woods covered in naught but a poncho?"

"It wasn't a poncho. It was a tunic."

"My mistake." The young master adopted a faint smile when I corrected him. "Still. Please explain."

I had tried to explain to him what had happened – that I was born to another world and reincarnated here upon my prior death. I tried to tell him of both the divine blessing and curse. I trusted him for some reason enough to reveal my secrets. But that is not what he heard.

Clifford's cheeks were turning a bright pink, and he began laughing uncontrollably. "So they just left you there? Naked? In the woods?" He almost fell out of his chair in laughter. "However incredible your story is, I can't imagine any man making one up like that. And while it doesn't answer everything, I am beginning to see why your skills are so underdeveloped. I do hope the gambling won't be a problem for us."

I was confused, not sure what he had heard when I told my story.

The young master determined that I would be most fit for any and all everyday tasks. I was all right with this. It afforded me some semblance of freedom. I could leave the grounds to go to the market, tend the garden and the stables, and do any odd job that needed a helping hand.

This gave me plenty of time to think, meet and talk to slaves from other houses, and learn the lay of the land.

I discovered that the entrapment barrier was fed nightly by hundreds of mages in the company palace. It was a spell of dark magic, fueled by the divine power of Mannana – the second time the death god has slighted me. The same magic infused in the fires and the brand that the masters owned. This is what the slaves called the oligarchs in private. "The masters."

The mark was less of a brand and more of a rune. When the entrapment barrier and the rune met, it activated a magical blood poison that quickly reduced HP at twice the loss of the person's HP pool upon being branded. This loss, they said, occurred in less than 30 seconds – meaning a slave could enjoy 30 seconds of freedom before death. Some had tried to cheat this by cutting the brand out of the skin, but doing so triggered it instantly.

Others earned their freedom from benevolent masters. The cost of liberty? 1000 gold per level above and beyond the initial purchase price, and the master's verbal consent in front of a certified bailiff. In our case, I learned that our master was technically Lord Clifford Grey. It was his brand we wore. And it was his first order as our master to bind us to his son. In our case, both father and son needed to consent to freedom. It didn't matter, though. Freeing myself and the Thane family would cost well beyond our current lifetime earning power. There was also the question of consent. That was not going to happen. Ever. Lord Clifford was known to be lawful neutral. He obeyed the laws in everything but did not hesitate to act in his self-interest whenever legal. He was an oligarch, after all. And one did not become a member of the elite class by being charitable.

I learned one thing, most of all. While our master was benevolent and had guards who were slow to the lash, others didn't share the same fortune. Many were beaten only because their owners enjoyed it. Families were separated. Wives, girls, and boys were sold as whores. Children were often sold to mining guilds as punishment for disobedient parents. Men, women, and children were all raped by some of the more cruel masters. And masters juggled slaves between themselves like a clown would juggle bowling pins. And at each slave exchange, the mark was painfully erased and re-branded.

Because it took me a week to learn what I could about Vros and Elatha, it took me more time to create my inspired escape plan. Sitting in a room with Cilden, Moga, Rose, and others from our group, I put all of my cards on the table:

"I know I may look weak. I'm only level 3, and my skills are undeveloped, but I have knowledge. I know how we can escape. And not just us. Hundreds of us."

A deafening silence filled our small lounge. If my ears were ringing from the silence any louder, the ringing would have woken the children in the next room.

"Impossible, Mike." Even in a week, Cilden and I had become fast friends. I spared him and his wife a few lashings by tending to the children while they performed their duties – Cilden in the garden and his wife in the kitchen.

"Not impossible. Not at all. Just… difficult. I'm going to need all of you to help. Rose – I know you're not going to like this – but I will need Neeta and Junta to help as well."

Rose pushed back from the table, roaring with motherly protection, the thought of involving her children unacceptable. I quickly continued.

"They will not be in danger, but they are the most important part of this plan. As children, they can get what I need without anyone seeing them as more than a nuisance."

I continued to lay out the plot in great detail. To get to the barrier, we needed a distraction. The masters often have meetings and parties with no slaves in attendance. Apparently, they had secrets that idle ears should not hear. When we are ready, we could act during one of these events.

I would need a significant number of invisibility potions. Four flasks per escaping slave. We would need each slave to have one or two healing potions. And we would need a dozen slaves trained in casting Healing Touch.

"But Michael," Rose called me Michael when she was upset with me. The woman was slow to be my friend. "You don't know how to cast healing touch. And I can't teach it. You certainly don't know how to make an invisibility potion."

"Moon grass, jasmine flower, wisp root, and water. I know how to make it. We just need to increase our Herbalism skill enough to be successful. Add a drop of blood from the imbiber and go to town. One hour of complete invisibility unless damage is taken. You can make it quick by biting your cheek to draw blood before you drink it."

"Why would we go to town?" Moga asked. I laughed a little, explaining that it was an expression from my homeland.

Rose looked at me in disbelief. She didn't know if I spoke the truth, but I think my Leadership skill triggered. She ended her fervent pacing and sat back down.

"As for you teaching us how to heal. You're not going to like this. Last week you said 'unless someone was willing to mutilate himself.' Well… I'm someone. Whenever we have the chance, I will willingly harm myself for you to heal me. It's going to suck, but we will get you to rank 30, so you can teach me that spell."

The plan dumbfounded the group. "Once we're ready, the core group of us, the children, the healers, and their families will all escape using the invisibility potions. I've already scoured the outskirts of the barrier when I've gone to the outer markets. We can station ourselves at random positions and pass through the barrier one at a time. Since I am the lowest level, I will go first. I can offset the damage over time spell with a strong healing potion. I know the ingredients and will have to make hundreds of them until I can raise my skill enough to make the invisibility flasks. Once I am through, you and the other healers will follow. An hour later, the rest of the slaves should arrive. We will use lesser healing potions and Healing Touch to keep them alive. We can then flee to a safe place – where we can remain hidden, gain strength, and secure passage out of this ass-backwards country."

They all looked at me in confusion. I needed to avoid using slang from home. It didn't translate here.

"I'm not going to lie. Some may not survive the barrier, especially those who had a high constitution before being branded." I paused to give Moga a sorrowful look. He was the highest level among us and had built up his Constitution as a hunter. He needed the stamina. He understood that I meant him, but was unfazed by it. His tight-lipped frown remained unchanged "That is why we have to get the message out. All slaves need to begin leveling themselves and adding their attribute points to their constitution. The more health they have, the better."

Rose was calm again. "Okay. I understand. It's a good plan. Insane, but good. What do you need the children to do?"

"Get me as many herbs as possible. Moon grass, jasmine, wisp root, and ginseng. We have a bigger problem, though. How are we all going to level here? We can't exactly increase our level substantially by killing cellar mice and cockroaches." I felt a cockroach crunch under my foot.

Moga spoke up for the first time that evening. "Why don't you just issue quests?"

"You can do that?!"

Everyone was struck dumb in disbelief at my ignorance. They still weren't sure what to make of me.

Vindur chimed in. "If you have a challenging goal, which you do, you can create any number of daily or ad-hoc quests for those involved in accomplishing this aim. Now a husband can't make a quest for his wife to cook dinner. That's too easy. The gods won't care. But quests to achieve a widespread slave rebellion will certainly result in quests that earn a decent amount of XP."

When Vindur was done inundating me with his tardy information, I turned back to the group.

"Nevermind. Let's do this. We have to be crazy careful, though." Another turn of phrase they didn't completely understand. I shrugged it off. "If we all start leveling up like dungeon delvers, I doubt the masters will ignore it. We should only instruct those who were a higher level when being branded to gain one or two levels. The group of us can pick up a level or two. The children should each get two or three. We can't raise any suspicion."

Congratulations! You have shown remarkable insight as a leader. Your skill in leadership has increased to rank 2!

...

Congratulations! You have shown remarkable insight as a leader. Your skill in leadership has increased to rank 5!

Congratulations! Your solid plan has impressed Moga. Your disposition with him has increased from Unfriendly to Indifferent.

Congratulations! Your care for the well-being of the Thane children has earned the gratitude of Cilden. Your disposition with him has increased from Friendly to Trusted.

Congratulations! Your care for the well-being of the Thane children has earned the respect of Rose. Your disposition with her has increased from Neutral to Friendly.

I looked at the ranks of disposition for the first time: Enemy, hated, unfriendly, indifferent, neutral, friendly, trusted, ally, companion. There were more disposition ranks now. The game only had five. Indifferent, enemy, ally, and companion were new. Vindur enlightened me about my only question. Indifferent was negative. Someone didn't like you, but they didn't disregard you. Those who were neutral had no opinion and treated you like they would a stranger, which could be either a good or bad thing depending on the person.

6

With the meeting over, everyone returned to their rooms. I decided to escape to the garden for a midnight stroll. I still had to procure samples of the herbs the children would need to make our plan work. They were instrumental in our success and, if everything worked out, they would have the makings of promising herbalists in the future.

I always loved Herbalism in Fjorgyn Online. Unlike other games that separated gathering professions and crafting ones, Fjorgyn combined the two. It made more sense. Herbalists knew the properties of herbs. Why would they have to level both herbalism and alchemy separately? Tailors needed cloth. Why couldn't they just get it and make what they needed?

Procuring materials was a solid way to level the profession. I still couldn't waste time doing it if I was going to make hundreds of potent potions for our potential slave rebellion while constantly mutilating myself for the sake of Rose's healing skill. The thought of my commitment to injure myself over and over and over again made my stomach churn. I was sure there had to be a better way, but no freeman or slave owner was going to willingly teach us how to heal ourselves.

I examined a jasmine bud and gently separated a stalk from the main stem. If the children were going to do this, they would have to make sure not to strip the garden bare. I had to talk to them about picking the essential ingredient without destroying the plant.

Congratulations! You have discovered a new skill! Herbalism. You can use natural ingredients to brew powerful potions and poisons! Increase in rank to create more potent concoctions and for greater success in making more complex solutions. Current rank: 1 (2%)

"You know why we plant so much jasmine, right?" A voice penetrated the shadows of the darker-than-usual night. Squinting at the source, I saw the outline of the young Clifford Grey. "We don't need it for healing potions. The scent calms everyone, including slaves. The miasma reduces tensions that can lead to rebellion." He paused only to step out of the shadows. "I know what you're all up to."

I shuffled back and fell to the ground, afraid that our plan would be revealed and our lives would be forfeit before we even got started. Vindur fell from my shoulder and circled around the garden to get a better look at Clifford Grey. I tried to speak, but words failed me.

"No, no, no. I'll have none of that. Stand up." I obeyed, looking him in the eyes. I had to tilt my head upwards. As a Trisian, he had at least one foot on me.

"You, my dear slaves, are planning an escape. And if I heard you right, you're planning on bringing more than just fifteen of you along. Now this plan of yours will most likely fall into ruin, but I like it and I want to help."

I felt as though I had finally seen Clifford Grey for the first time. The layers of "owner of slaves" peeled away slightly to show a calmer, more enlightened man. He was nothing like this father. What I first thought was cockiness and entitlement suddenly became strength and influence. I still had my reservations.

"Why would you help us? You're a master. You've built your entire civilization on the backs of slaves. You own us."

"Because I don't want to own you! I don't want there to be masters and slaves. Believe it or not, Vros wasn't always like this. We were once a proud people and had an empire that spanned the entire continent.

The wealthy always had paid servants, but never slaves... Now we have become complacent. Look around you. We hide behind our protective barriers and walls, wasting away in our putrid gardens while monopolizing trade goods. We haven't discovered a new potion or enchantment or spell in over a century! We milk from the poor and lounge around all day and it has made us fat and lazy and cruel."

"You're not fat or lazy, master."

"Well, I take pride in that. My father, however, does not share my appreciation for healthy living and hard work. Anyhow, I heard your plan in full, and I want to make it work. Hundreds of slaves escaping is just the leverage this nation needs to inspire change in leadership." He paced back and forth, his tense muscles stretching out his shirt. He brushed his hands through his hair, lost in deep thought for a moment. "If you haven't noticed, we have a hierarchy based on merit. And if those in charge suddenly misplace hundreds of slaves in a single night, events will be set in motion to enact positive change. The upset will create a vacuum of power that can be leveraged by those wanting abolition."

As his words sunk in, I reviewed our plan in my head.

"I think we have everything covered for the moment."

A chortle escaped his lips. "Silly man. You have nothing 'covered.' Take whatever herbs you need from my garden. I certainly cannot produce what you will need. I will purchase the rest. I will also have a thousand vials brought to the basement. You can brew to your heart's content now that I see you have the skill." He was referring to my careful attention to the jasmine plant.

"And when you identify those slaves who will serve as healers, I will attempt to buy them. They will certainly need a place to be trained outside of the scrutiny of an attentive master. As for the rest, I will see that a small portion of them are equipped with weapons from my personal stockpile when they reach the barrier – but not before. I will not arm an insurrection within this city. I saw the look in your eyes during our personal introduction. You corrected me like an equal, like one who does not think himself a slave. You wanted rebellion. Let us make that happen in the future, but only once they are free."

I was taken aback at all of the things I overlooked. Every word Clifford said was correct. We needed his help. And there was something about him that made me want to trust and follow him. This must be what others felt when their disposition towards me change.

"There's a catch, though." That trust quickly wavered. Why was there always a catch?

"There is a small group of us who are friendly to your cause. We were forced to be masters by our parents. We would see ourselves free of this moral burden. While there is a faction of non-slave owners in the oligarchy who will further our plans, we will not escape blame when we allow our slaves to escape. You must take us with you."

That was fair. I offered silent consent.

"And I will have none of this self-mutilation nonsense. That's how blood magic is born. Your plan would require you stab yourself violently thousands of times before Rose reached level 30. This is a city of magic. Low-level healing spells are very expensive but can still be found in small numbers if you know where to look. Come to my library in the morning. Most people don't sell them. Most don't even make them for others. I can give you ten various healing spells that will work. I know the barrier. Rose's direct healing touch is alright, but you also need more variety on top of health potions. And you need two healers per station. I won't have the barrier be littered with corpses in the morning because one person fails to cast in time."

Clifford produced a book from his inventory and tossed it towards me. "This one is for you."

Spell Tome: Healing Seed I. This spell plants a living seed in the body of the target that heals for 1hp per second for 10 seconds. Upon expiration, the target is healed for another 5hp. Mana cost: 20. Cast time: 2.5 seconds.

Without thinking, I rapidly turned the pages of the book. It took on a life of its own. A green glow exploded from the pages while the book turned to dust.

Congratulations! You have learned a new spell! Healing Seed I. This spell plants a living seed in the body of the target that heals for 1hp per second for 10 seconds. Upon expiration, the target is healed for another 5hp. The healing amount is augmented by wisdom. Mana cost: 20. This will increase in rank every five skill levels, improving the healing value and increasing the mana cost.

I must have been brimming with joy when reading the notification. I quickly cast the spell on myself, and a soft green tendril emanated from the center of my chest before vanishing. I could feel the mana reduction. It made me dizzy. I also felt healing power wash over my entire body. The spells power was reduced by my loss in base wisdom. I had to gain a few levels to make the spell more powerful.

"I can see your gears turning and know what you're thinking. You – all fifteen of you – have my permission to level to your heart's content. I cannot promise the same for my father. If he shows up, ensure that he is only served by the lowest level among you. He should not notice a slave gaining one or two levels. That is insignificant. He seems to have remembered you, though. If he notices that you are leveling quickly, he will have you killed."

"Master, thank you." The young man put his hand on my shoulder and offered me a reassuring nod. There was also a spark of something else in his eyes. Something I couldn't put my finger on. "I mean it. Thank you."

Congratulations! Your trust in Clifford Grey II has improved your relationship. Your disposition with him has increased from Indifferent to Neutral.

Clifford turned around and left the garden without another word.
"What do you think, Vindur?"
"I believe you are one lucky elf."
I was beaming with a new hope, rushing back to the basement to tell the others. Rose was amazed at my new spell and my aptitude with it. She even admitted that she was unsure if I would have taken to her divine healing spell seeing how quickly I was able to cast nature-based healing.
They all agreed with one thing, though. If this plan was to have any

chance of succeeding, the core group of them would have to do everything they could to level up. They all had to become healers. I had to make more potions than most people made in their entire lives. We had to escape with resources enough not only to survive but to thrive. We had to become a company.

The next morning felt like a bright, new day. For the first time in over two weeks, my new friends had a sense of hope. They had been given the green flag from their master to increase their level and plant the seeds for a slave rebellion. Over breakfast, I explained to the children the proper method for picking herbs, showing them the difference between slowly removing the essential components and ripping the plant to shreds.

Rose warned the two to be careful, to not be seen harvesting herbs in other gardens and to remain within the confines of their estate. After the two had stuffed their faces with toast and eggs, they accepted the quests we had given them and ran off, eager to test their new skills.

I fiddled with my own breakfast: a single slice of toast, a fried egg, and a few bits of bacon. Now that we were on more friendly terms, Clifford saw fit to provide us food that would fill our bellies, unlike other households where slaves were forced to operate on 75% fatigue. A few minutes later, with time to spare before I had to meet him, I decided to wash up. I hadn't been keeping myself nearly as clean as I should have, mostly because I was pissed off at being locked away as a slave.

Vindur and I headed to the washroom. I wanted to leave him behind but he refused. Last time he sent me away on my own, I was captured and sold into slavery.

The washroom was simple. It had a single sink (working plumbing did cheer me up), small stools, buckets, soap, and rags. Any water poured on the floor drained into a small hole in the center of the room to be reclaimed, filtered by the soil and sand beneath us, and recycled again to the nearest well.

The room was intended to serve everyone, but we had a standing agreement that men would clean in the morning and women would clean in the afternoon. It was offered as a place of seclusion in the evening for anyone who wished to use it at night. Already, the rest of the group had washed aside from Baridorne, a level 9 half-giant that had been brought here with us.

Analyzing Baridorne yielded impressive results. He was 43 years old, possessing a high skill in heavy armor and two-handed weapons – rank 13 in both. He also had the same builder, agriculture, and creature of burden ranks as Cilden. What surprised me most of all were the scars on his back. A spider web of thin lines covered his entire back-side, some wrapping around his torso to mark his ribs. I pieced together his story from this information alone. He must have been a soldier fighting Vros, only to be captured by slavers.

"I escaped before they were able to brand me." Baridorne broke the silence. "You were going to ask that, right?"

His voice echoed in the room – a deep and booming voice that commanded respect.

"Yes, I was." Pleased with my honesty, Baridorne resumed cleaning himself. Stripping off my clothes, I took the stool next to him and began washing with a small bit of rag dipped in a soapy bucket. The man was a behemoth next to me, easily eight feet tall.

"We're all going to get out of this, you know. I believe in your plan." The man's words were comforting. Despite trusting to hope, I worried that I would let my new friends down. I experienced this same doubt on earth and in the game whenever I was afforded the chance to lead. I often failed on earth. And in the game, failure was always an option. If I lost, I could resurrect and try again. This wasn't earth, where a loss meant money out of my pocket. This wasn't a game, either. What I was planning had real consequences for hundreds of people. I would resurrect. They could all die.

"You have all trusted in me despite my low level and my having no apparent and useful skills. Rose and Cilden trust me with their children. You and Moga and the others trust me with your lives. Why?"

"Because, boss. You're the only one giving us a chance." The half-giant pushed up from his stools and turned towards me. I quickly learned that he was large. Everywhere. I stood up to meet him only to avoid staring at his oversized junk. His eyes were puffy. He had been crying. "Can you promise me something?" he asked.

Before I could accept, he continued: "When the guards came, I held them off while my wife and daughter escaped into the forest. She is only level 6 and my daughter is only a newborn. We just named her that day, after my mother, Una. When we get out of here, will you help me find them?"

You have received a quest! "Family Bonds."
Baridorne has asked you to help him locate his missing wife and child.
Reward: Experience gain and disposition gain with Baridorne.
Bonus: Find them alive and in good health for an additional, unknown
   reward.

"There is no possible way I could say no to your request. I accept, my friend."

A massive grin exploded on his face. He couldn't contain himself and picked me up in a skin-on-skin bear hug. I could feel my spine cracking as he embraced me in relief and excitement before putting me back down. He thanked me profusely before planting me back on my feet. He rushed out of the room, too happy to remember his towel. Rose started screaming in the hallway, yelling at Baridorne to get dressed. Something about "There are children around!" and "Put that away before I cut it off!" and "Put me down! I don't want a hug! Michael! What did you do!?"

Congratulations! Your expression of selflessness has inspired
   Baridorne to no end. Your disposition with him has increased from
   Neutral to Trusted. Continue building your relationship with him
   and you will gain a true ally.

I was left alone in the room with Vindur. He was drinking from the basin in the back of the room, struggling to reach the water.

"Vindur, why are you a crow?" I asked him.

"Because I wanted to be."

"Can't you be something else?" It was an honest question. A bird wasn't the most useful form in the world. He couldn't climb things, he couldn't eat or drink easily. I massaged my shoulder thinking of his nails biting into my skin.

"Absolutely." A cloud of smoke enveloped him. Feathers gave way to fur. His beak was replaced with a nose and whiskers. When the smoke vanished, he was now a black cat. Pleased with his transformation, he was now able to easily reach the water.

"That's not any better. How about something more? How about a lemur?"

Vindur shrugged in response to my question. "If that will make you happy." The process repeated again. The results were more pleasing to me. He was now a gray lemur with a white face and a black and white, striped tail. His ears also matched mine, forming a gentle point at their tip. I could now read the expressions on his face as well. And he looked both bored and frustrated.

"Much better. Thank you."

7

This was the second time I had been in Clifford's study. It was the largest room in the house. Three walls were dedicated only to book storage, broken down into an endless number of categories: spell work, herbalism, enchanting, religion and religious history, politics and law, history, and even a section dedicated to fiction. "The She-Elf and the Pixie King" was one title that caught my eye. I wonder if Fjorgyn has developed fantasy-erotica since my rebirth. What did fantasy erotica look like in a fantasy world?

The front of the room was furnished with sofas and a coffee table stacked high with recently used books and a bowl of fresh fruit. Behind it, two chairs faced an oversized desk where Clifford was sitting. Behind him, there was a fireplace so large that one could walk into it. If it weren't on fire, that is.

Vindur jumped off my shoulder and started stuffing his face with grapes. I was pleased with his new form. A lemur was much funnier than a crow. I let him indulge himself and stepped further into the room, attempting to hide my amazement with the sheer number of tomes available.

"Michael, good morning." Clifford motioned for me to sit down. I hesitated, tugging on my leather collar. The thing itched my skin something fierce, like a horny frat boy with crabs.

"No, master. I'm fine standing."

"I'll have none of that. I thought we agreed last night. There are no masters here."

"We did. And I am grateful, but I want to maintain the pretense. Prying eyes and all." I gestured to the window. Even with the walls, there was nothing preventing people outside of them from seeing into his study.

"So be it. I have two tasks for you today that will help both of us. First, I have need of an escort to a High Protectorate meeting. Not only will this give me a safe excuse to give you some armor, but it will shed more light on how things work here in Elatha, something you somehow seem completely oblivious about. And you have been walking around barefoot for a week now. It's embarrassing." He pointed at a pile of armor resting on a nearby chair.

Rough Leather Chestpiece. Quality: Good. Class: Uncommon. Armor: Light(15). Stats: +10 HP

Homespun Pants. Quality: Good. Class: Uncommon. Armor: Light(10). Stats: +20 MP

Leather boots. Quality: Good. Class: Uncommon. Armor: Light(5). Stats: +10% movement speed

Leather bracers. Quality: Good. Class: Uncommon. Armor: Light(5). Stats: +10 HP

I must have drooled because Clifford started laughing again. Unbecoming of his station, he helped me put the armor on. I took care of changing out of my pants, folding them gently and putting them in my inventory. They were still a gift that could be put to a purpose. And every gamer was a secret hoarder.

"I'd give you a weapon as well, but we would both be killed if I were to provide one to a slave. I am, however, making you my valet. If anyone should ask your position, that's it. Now let's go. The meeting is in an hour." His behavior had changed. He is less formal than yesterday. The young man was more relaxed and more familiar with me, and

I noticed how handsome he truly was. When he was helping me with my armor, I had felt like a knight and him my squire. I tried my hardest not to blush, hoping he would ignore the now obvious attraction I had started feeling toward him.

> *You have received a quest! "Errands, errands everywhere!" Clifford Grey II has asked you to accompany him while completing two errands. He is your master. This quest is non-optional.*
> *Reward: Experience gain and disposition gain with Clifford Grey II*

As we were walking, I asked about the second task. Clifford dismissed my questions like a master would in public. I would have to wait and see. Instead, he explained more about the meeting.

"It's unusual for slaves to be included in these meetings. When they are, the tendency is to armor your slaves temporarily with the same armor provided to initiate guards." I must have looked sad while I rubbed the soft leather of my new chest piece. Clifford chuckled. "Don't worry. Those are yours to keep. They'll come in handy later."

"Anyhow, this meeting is for all of the masters in the city. The High King, head of the Wraithheart company, will be issuing an edict. He doesn't do this often. When he does, attendance by one member of the each master's household is compulsory. My father is away on business and will be gone for the next few months... this also works in our favor."

He stopped at the base of the stairs to the central palace as masters and slaves filed by us. The building was massive, easily eight stories tall and a thousand feet wide. It loomed over the city as a symbol of unchecked power. The staircase leading up to it was at least five stories with guard stations posted at each landing. It reminded me of the Vatican City, although I only know from pictures.

"Michael, this is important. You will be asked to show your mark. Do not hesitate. When we are inside, you must always stand behind me and to my right side. You must not speak to me unless spoken to first. You must look to me for permission should anyone ask you a question beyond 'Show me your mark.' And you must not, under any circumstance, talk to another slave."

I nodded my understanding although his instructions triggered apprehension. I was about to enter the heart of darkness. Quite literally. The power within fed the barrier that clouded the entire city in an endless night.

"And before I forget, you need to carry this." He handed me his inventory bag and willed it into my possession. I examined the contents with my mind, second nature whenever receiving a new item. It contained various herbs, potions, scrolls, armor and weapons, and leather bound books. He had an 80-slot inventory! To my 20.

"A master cannot be seen carrying anything within the palace with a slave present. And this," he tapped on the bag, "I expect back."

The thought never crossed my mind. Okay. It crossed my mind once. But I wouldn't steal another person's inventory. Your inventory is an extension of yourself. It would be cruel.

Hiking up the stairs with two inventories and the weight of leather armor was terrible. My stamina decreased. My fatigue increased. The walk up did get easier, however. I had adjusted both inventories appropriately and saw notifications pop up in the corner of my eye.

Congratulations! Your skill as a Creature of Burden has increased to rank 6. Heavy loads are now 3% lighter.
Congratulations! Your skill as a Creature of Burden has increased to rank 7. Heavy loads are now 3.5% lighter.

I could feel the muscles in my back and legs strengthen when my skill increased. My stamina decreased at a much slower rate. I no longer felt out of breath when we reached the top and my fatigue amount had begun to decline again.

"Vindur, what's the difference between stamina and fatigue?"

Vindur obliged with what might have been one of the first world-related questions I asked him in a while. I could no longer blame him for tardy information. I had to begin asking more. This was not the game. Things in this world were different.

"Stamina reduces. Fatigue increases. You use Stamina when you run, exert yourself, or fight. If you run out of it, you can collapse. Fatigue increases through regular exertion or from not eating, sleeping, or drinking. If you reach 100% fatigue, you become over-encumbered. Walking can be a chore. Stamina and Mana do not regenerate, and health will not regenerate over time until you solve whatever is causing you to fatigue. The more fit you become, the slower your fatigue increases."

His was a perfect explanation. I scolded myself for not thinking of asking before.

At the top of the stairs, massive wooden doors stood open. They had to be thirty feet high. The inside of the building was lit by enchanted torches that illuminated a white light, almost as though they were operating on electricity. For the first time in a week, I felt as though I was walking into daylight again. I silently cursed the masters for what I saw was another sign of oppression. They allowed themselves to live in the light while the people they should be protecting served their interests in darkness.

The décor was red and gold. It was tacky and stunk of self-importance. We shuffled through the main corridor into a central chamber. In the front of the over-sized room, there was a row of nine chairs all decreasing in size and comfort. The central chair was a pillowed throne cast in gold. The outer seats were wooden kitchen chairs with red leather backing and seating.

The room itself was an auditorium split into four levels; a ringed auditorium within a ringed city, another way to divide people into groups within groups. This was another sign of company oppression. As we were walking, a guard stopped us and had me show him my mark. Pleased with the size and severity of it, he waved us on.

Clifford led me to his assigned section in the second ring. The room was at capacity. Thousands of masters and slaves congregated, all of us wearing some semblance of leather armor colored to match the sigil of the house we served. My armor was green with silver thread and had a silver owl printed on the chest piece. The masters of the outer ring wore everyday clothes. Many of them were dirty. I assumed they had purchased slaves after a significant amount of saving to supplement their workforce.

The third ring consisted of merchants and those of higher-paying professions. Even then, their clothing was unremarkable.

The second ring consisted of minor aristocrats. The masters of this ring, save Clifford, were mostly older and more rotund. The inner ring consisted of fat men in fancy dress with slaves adorned in various degrees of impractical armor meant more to show off their wealth than to provide protection. They were the one ring with chairs to sit in. Many did sit out of necessity, weighed down by years of gluttony. Some slaves were fanning their masters. Others were holding silver or gold chalices. I could swear that I even saw a few powdered wigs. These were the top of the aristocrats who had accumulated more money and wealth than the rest combined.

The room grew silent when a gong resounded through the chamber. Older men filed in from behind a curtain and took their place in the outer chairs on the stage. Trumpets sang when a young man walked out and took his place on the throne. He was dressed in black robes that glimmered like the evening sky. I thought I saw shooting stars fly across the fabric. A red collar poked out of the top of the robes to match his blood-red hair. It all stood in stark contrast to his abnormally pale skin, broken only by some runic tattoos on his forehead and cheekbone. He carried a staff that was thin, smooth, and black. Affixed to the staff was a cradle that contained a diamond the color of midnight. I analyzed him quickly:

Name: Ankou Levent
Title: High King of Vros
Race: Trisian - ???
Age: 143
Class: Mage
Talent: Necromancy, Elemental
Level: ???
Health: ???
Mana: ???
Stamina: ???
Alignment: Lawful evil (+100)
Profession: Herbalist, Enchanter, Crafting, Inscription
Disposition: Unfriendly
Company: Wraithheart (Leader)

I retreated, afraid, after analyzing the high king. Clifford gripped my arm and pulled me closer to his side, silently instructing me not to waver in Levent's presence. The High King inspired many questions. Why couldn't I see his level? Why was his biracial status hidden? How was he so young in appearance while so old in age? How did he secure multiple talents and professions? I was afraid of this man, more afraid than I have been of anything in my entire life. And I knew nothing about him beyond his aura of death and destruction and power.

With High King Levent seated, the room fell silent. You could almost hear the beads of sweat hitting the floor from nervous masters and slaves alike. Levent slammed the bottom of his staff into the ground, reverberations echoing through the auditorium. The white-flame sconces on the wall extinguished leaving only the middle of the room illuminated. The area in front of the high king slid open and a platform ascended. Chained to the floor was a Trisian man, woman, a little girl, and some slaves. They cowered before their king. The scent of them filled the large auditorium – one of shit and urine and sweat and musk.

Without standing, Levent spoke: "My compatriots, I've called you here today to raise charges against a fellow company member. The man you see before you was one of my chief advisors and my friend. I need not give you his name. It has been stricken from history. He and his entire household are charged with high treason. Their crime? Attempting to skirt the natural order of our great and powerful nation by plotting to escape to another country."

The audience gasped at this revelation. I didn't understand it until I realized that this was a police state that forbade foreign refuge.

"Nameless man, how do you plead?"

The man was shaken to his core, unable to look up at the high king who was lounging lazily on his throne. He whispered something for his king to hear.

"I don't think they heard you. Louder."

More mumbling.

"Louder!"

The man's head shot upright, and he screamed for all to hear.

"Mercy!"

Levent exploded from his chair and slammed his staff into the ground. Shockwaves rippled across the room, and many fell to their knees. I almost would have if Clifford were not still clutching my arm. At this point, we were trembling in unison.

"You are my child! You are all my children! I have given you every-thing in exchange for obedience! You," he pointed a bony finger at the man and his family, "sought to take that away from me! You shall have no mercy!"

His slender hand waved over the prisoners. They all went stiff as the king's dark magic washed over them. One by one their bodies straightened, and they lifted off the ground with only the tips of their toes touching.

"I am your Lord! I called you my friend only for you to betray me! I am the black of night! I am the Lion of Elatha! I am judge, jury, and executioner! You, nameless-one, and your family are hereby sentenced to undergo my death rite. This is my judgment, and as such, it is beyond contestation!"

The crowd began to erupt in chants and applause. Some shouted at their lord and master "Great is the lion!" and "Our King is just and wise!" The masters in the room began beating their hands against their chests, Clifford included, chanting "Lion, Lion, Lion."

After a minute of chanting, Levent raised his staff. The crowd grew silent. Still gripping the prisoners in the air, he pointed his staff at them and whispered inaudible words of dark power. A plume of black smoke billowed from the diamond and enveloped them. I caught glimpses of them struggling and screaming as the smog enveloped them in a small cyclone. I could hear no cries. First, they were clothed. Then they were naked. Then the flesh eroded from their bones. The bones began to crack and break leaving only a pure, blue light. All the while, the dark magic kept them aware and alive, writhing in inaudible agony.

The smoked stopped spinning and retreated into the staff again. All that remained of the prisoners were their souls. With the smoke gone, I could now hear their cries again, leaving my heart shattered. Tears began to form in my eyes. One by one, the blue lights began to fade. That is until Levent stepped forward and prodded them with his staff, absorbing each spirit into the diamond. The last orb was the smallest. The king walked circles around it. I could hear it calling out. "Mommy? Mommy where are you? I don't know where I am. Where are you, mommy?"

The king was taken aback by the child's cry for help. He watched the light grow dimmer and dimmer until he placed his free hand on it and lifted it up to the sky, releasing the soul to the gods.

"Know this," he said after the ritual was complete. "I love you all. You are all my children. As such, you should be aware of the truth. The world outside of Vros is dark and dangerous. Demons and monsters roam Fjorgyn. These foreign invaders will seek to destroy us. This morning I learned that we are the last great and powerful Trisian empire. We must remain faithful and unwavering. I command the borders to be sealed. The first-born son or daughter of every household is hereby conscripted, save those who are only children. There will be no exceptions. We will meet this alien threat. We will see victory."

The room erupted again with praises of their Lord, lover of innocence and children: protector of all. The applause continued for ten minutes, long after Levent and the High Protectorate left the room.

When the auditorium became illuminated, people began to file out. Some were still applauding. Some were on their knees crying, both in terror and joy. And Clifford was still standing there gripping my now bruised forearm. The silhouette of his face showed a man mustering every ounce of restraint to suppress unwavering hatred.

I stood behind him silently for a few more minutes while he regained himself. He turned around and locked eyes with me. Hatred faded. It was replaced with determination and hope and something else that I hadn't seen in him before.

8

We walked in silence, a silence so tense you could cut it with a knife. Clifford was shaken to his core. I followed behind him as we walked through the inner city and into the outer rings, most likely on our way to his second task for the day. I analyzed him for the first time:

Name: Clifford Grey II
Title: Earl
Race: Trisian
Age: 31
Class: Warrior
Talent: Protection
Level: 17
Health: 235
Mana: 160
Stamina: 220
Alignment: Chaotic good (+11)
Profession: Scholar
Disposition: Trusted
Company: Wraithheart (Junior Member)

His Disposition towards me was different. Last time we spoke, it had changed to neutral. I pulled up my notifications.

Congratulations! Your skill in observation has increased to rank 3.
Know this! You have witnessed a unique event of profound dark power in the heart of a city. Your race has been modified from 'Forest Elf' to 'Dark Elf.' You are now less at home in the forest and more suited for cities. -10% damage and healing during the day. +10% damage and healing at night and in dark places.
Congratulations! Your skill in observation has increased to rank 4.
Congratulations! Your skill in observation has increased to rank 5.
Congratulations! Your skill in observation has increased to rank 6.
Congratulations! Your unwavering support of Clifford Grey II during an emotional crisis has improved your relationship. Your disposition with him has increased substantially from Neutral to Trusted.

I didn't understand the observation skill. Increasing my rank didn't improve anything. It was generic, like the Luck attribute. I was pleased with my relationship with Clifford. He was a good man and we share common convictions. As his disposition toward me increased, so did mine toward him.

"You look sickly. Are you alright?" Clifford had at last broken the silence when we crossed to the outer ring of the city, trudging through mud and slums to get to our mysterious destination.

"No, I'm not," I said. It was the truth. Not only had I witnessed the murder of an innocent child. I had also been transformed into a different race. My skin lost its glow. It had become more translucent and pale. And my hair had lost its brown luster and was dull and plain.

"Whatever Leve-"

"Don't say his name out loud."

"Whatever he did… it changed me. I'm a dark elf now. I feel violated."

"I'm sorry that I brought you. I should have known better than to bring an elf. Still. It isn't permanent. You can always change back. Where we're going should help."

I asked Vindur what he meant.

"Elves change. Because you haven't been a forest elf for that long, the change was easier. There's nothing wrong with it. It makes you adaptable. If you spend enough time in one place, you will transform."

We walked for two more hours along the inside perimeter of the barrier. Unlike when we arrived, the bubble was vibrating and buzzing. I could feel similar vibrations in my shoulder—the rune repelling itself from the dark shell surrounding Elatha. Walking down a ravine, we finally reached our destination: a cave entrance sporting a rough, wooden door.

Clifford reclaimed his inventory from me. Reaching into it, he pulled out a set of armor, a broadsword, and a shortsword. He also drew out a small dagger and a staff, sliding out of his inventory like Mary Poppins claimed her coat-rack. Inventories were funny. If you had the available space, you could fit anything into them. Want to carry forty plates? Sure. They stack.

"Take these." He handed me my weapons. As I held them, I was tense. "Don't worry. Guards never come this way. Few people do. No one wants to be this close to the barrier."

I tied the sheath around my thigh and held the staff in my hand. I examined both:

> *Fine steel dagger with sheath. Quality: Good. Class: Uncommon. Damage: 10-15 DPS. Can be broken by stronger weapons.*
> *Staff of Force Push. Quality: Professional. Class: Rare. Damage: 17-23 DPS. Can be broken by stronger weapons. Stats: +30 MP, chance to send shockwaves at a target to push it back. This is more effective against smaller enemies. It can also aid in deflecting weapon strikes. Can disrupt spellcasting. Charges: 97/100.*

I was going to say that the gifts were two much. I mean a rare quality item! Then I remembered that Clifford was an aristocrat. While I was appreciating my new staff, he had secured his armor and weapon and was ready to go. The man had transformed in front of my eyes, wearing armor as gray as slate. He wore a chainmail shirt and pants, a breastplate, greaves, pauldrons, and gauntlets. He looked like the adventurers I was used to seeing. Pulling up his information, I saw a remarkable improvement.

Name: Clifford Grey II
Title: Earl
Race: Trisian
Age: 31
Class: Warrior
Talent: Protection
Level: 17
Health: 674 (235)
Mana: 245 (160)
Stamina: 543 (220)
Alignment: Chaotic good (+11)
Profession: Scholar
Disposition: Trusted
Company: Wraithheart (Junior Member)

"Michael! Accept the party invite!" Being startled back to attention, I realized I was ignoring my notifications.

Clifford Grey II has invited you to join a party. Doing so will result in your sharing all money and experience earned in combat. Do you accept? Y/N"

I accepted without thinking. His still-open character screen exploded with more information:

Name: Clifford Grey II
Title: Earl
Race: Trisian

Age: 31
Class: Warrior
Talent: Protection
Level: 17
Health: 674 (235)
Mana: 245 (160)
Stamina: 543 (220)
Fatigue: 5%
Armor: 1123 (13.2% damage reduction) – 21% damage reduction with skills.
Magical resistance: 10%
Alignment: Chaotic good (+11)
Profession: Scholar
Disposition: Friendly
Company: Wraithheart (Junior Member)

Active weapon(s):

Broadsword of Fire strike. Quality: Exquisite. Class: Epic. Damage: 107-123 DPS. Can be broken by stronger weapons. Stats: 10% chance to set a target on fire. 10HP fire damage every second for 5 seconds. Charges: 91/100.
Restrictions: Warrior, level 17

Shortsword of Magical repulsion. Quality: Exquisite. Class: Rare. Damage: 52-61 DPS. Can be broken by stronger weapons. Status: 10% resistance to magic damage (passive).
Restrictions: Level 16

I held my excitement in when seeing the first epic weapon since my rebirth. It put my original rusty iron dagger to shame. I closed Clifford's interface and was now privy to the party view. I saw my health, mana, and stamina. Below that, I saw Clifford's health, mana and stamina and his current target, Vindur.

"What the hell is that?" Clifford yelled, arms at the ready.

I flew backward, almost crashing into the barrier. Clifford grabbed my hand and pulled me forward again.

"That is… he is… what I mean to say is…" I coughed to clear my throat and regained my balance. "He is Vindur, my ally and guide."

"Ally and guide? What do you mean? He can talk? He has been here the whole time? Why am I now just noticing him?He can talk!?"

"Clifford… I wish I could tell you, but I can't. One day I will. I promise. But you must learn to trust me more before then."

You have received a quest! "Furry Lemur and friends!"
Tell Clifford Grey II the story of your rebirth in Fjorgyn, and details about Vindur. This quest is non-optional. You promised. Words have meaning.
Criteria: He must become your ally.
Failure criteria: Clifford Grey II disposition reduction from Hated or Enemy or one year passes.
Reward: Experience gain, reputation gain

You have given a quest to Clifford Grey II! "Friend's furry lemur."
Reach disposition of companion with Michael Dian-Cecht. Michael Promised you the reward, making this quest non-optional.
Criteria: You become Michael's companion
Failure conditions: Michael's disposition towards you reduces to hated or enemy or one year expires.
Reward: Experience gain. Information on Michael's backstory and on his mysterious flying lemur.

White lines could be seen in Clifford's eyes as he read through the quest. He seemed smug and displeased with the shocking sight of the lemur. When we both dismissed the prompts, Vindur disappeared from Clifford's sight.

"Sorry, Michael. I'll double check my settings. I forgot to include party and raid members. Won't happen again."

"It better not," I said to him, frustration trembling in my throat. "Next time you scare someone like that, they might run me through."

After the excitement died down, Clifford led me into the dungeon. When we stepped through the shoddy doorway, the outside world vanished and the door slammed shut. Only the cavern wall remained.

Congratulations! You have found 'Nott's Sanctum'. Dungeon rank: Easy. Creature Class: Low intelligence. Level range: 5-13. +35xp

"Clifford, this is too high a level for me."

"No, it's not. I run my cousins through here all the time. They love it. I can get to the end on my own. I just want you to stay behind me and heal me when I take damage."

I felt apprehensive but trusted my new friend. He hadn't given me a reason not to. Well. Aside from owning me. Remembering my last battle, I willed my notifications into combat-mode. They wouldn't distract me again.

And so we pressed forward, crouching down as we moved. The cavern was narrow at first. After a few minutes it began to widen. Every ten to twenty feet a torch hung on the wall, illuminating the path in front of us. The deeper we went, the colder it became. We walked for five minutes when Clifford motioned for me to stop. Scurries, rattles, and squeaks echoed down the tunnel towards us.

"Rats. Joy. Why is it always rats?" I mumbled. I barely finished my complaining when the hairy creatures shuffled into view. I counted eight of them, all ranging between level 5 and 9 and having between 43 and 57 health.

They were aggravated by our presence and were targeting both of us. Clifford clanked his swords into the walls to grab their attention and they all rushed him at once. The rats lunged at him, finding their mark on various pieces of armor. One successfully scurried up his gauntlet and bit into his arm, teeth sharp enough to pierce his chain-mail. He didn't seem to mind or notice, only losing a few health.

For a warrior in heavy armor, he proved himself particularly agile. In one movement he pinned the rat on his arm against the wall and crushed it, inflicting damage and dropping it to the floor. He jumped back while jabbing both swords into two separate rats simultaneously. This movement confused me. It was one I'd only seen rogues perform. Dislodging his swords, his arms flew in a sweeping motion, points scraping the floor to create sparks. His broadsword enchantment triggered and a rat set on fire. It ran away in fear.

There was a pause in the battle as the bleeding rats reconstituted themselves. Three were dead, one had fled, but should die from the fire enchantment. I took this opportunity to cast Healing Seed on him. The spell took hold. A green tendril breached his wound before fading into his body. His health was returned to full and the wound had closed leaving only a bloodstain on his chainmail.

My healing spell didn't go unnoticed. One giant rat, still unharmed, scurried under Clifford's feet and tried to intercept me. Without hesitation, I punched the end of my staff into the creature and the enchantment triggered. The furry monster took the full force of the shockwave. It was propelled backwards ten feet, landing on its back in a daze.

I stepped forward to finish it off, but Clifford, having dispatched his targets, stepped forward and poked the beast with the tip of his shortsword, ending its short life.

He looked back at me with a smile. "That was quick thinking. You sure you never fought with a staff before?"

In this life, I never had. When I first played the game, the staff was my favorite weapon, although I never leveled the skill substantially. When I saved enough gold, I bought spells. They did all the work for me. As I advanced in level, I spent my time healing parties and raids, gathering supplies, crafting and running my company. I knew enough for rudimentary attacks and blocks, protecting myself long enough for someone else to draw a creature's attention away from me.

Clifford and I continued down the corridor, culling seven more hordes of rats. I became more comfortable with the staff as a weapon. I found the enchant to be useful. He showed me how to control it so it only triggered on command — I had to twist it slightly when I connected with my target, simulating a shock-wave that would trigger the magic. This allowed me to use the staff without exhausting the charges. He began to let more rats through his defenses. It was never more than two of the lowest level at a time. I took a few bites and scratches, but never for more than 10% of my total health. I was able to heal the damage to both of us with ease.

After an hour of fighting, our fatigue level had become high. We decided to break so I could scroll through my notifications.

Congratulations! You have discovered a new skill! Stave fighting. You can use staff weapons to both defend and attack your enemies. Increase in rank to increase damage and block amount! Current rank: 1 (1% increase damage, 1% increased chance of block).

You have killed a level 5 Cave Rat * 17. Penalty for high level support. 3 xp each. +51xp

You have killed a level 6 Cave Rat * 14. Penalty for high level support. 4 xp each. +56xp

You have killed a level 7 Cave Rat * 15. Penalty for high level support. 5 xp each. +75xp

You have killed a level 8 Cave Rat * 9. Penalty for high level support. 6 xp each. +54xp

You have killed a level 9 Cave Rat * 5. Penalty for high level support. Bonus for high-level kill. 10 xp each. +50xp

Congratulations! You have reached level 4! You have 2 attribute points to assign. 301xp to next level.

Congratulations! Your skill with staves has increased to rank 2. .1% additional damage when attacking. .2% additional chance to block.

Congratulations! You have gained rank 2 in Healing Seed I. .25% additional healing.

Congratulations! Your skill with light armor has increased to rank 2. 0.1% increase in damage mitigation and movement speed.

Congratulations! Your skill with stalking has increased to rank 2. .1% increase to stealth.

...

Congratulations! Your skill with staves has increased to rank 5. .1% additional damage when attacking. .2% additional chance to block.

Congratulations! Your skill with light armor has increased to rank 4. 0.1% increase in damage mitigation and movement speed.

Congratulations! Your skill with stalking has increased to rank 6. .1% increase to stealth

Congratulations! You have gained rank 5 in Healing Seed I. Spell

evolved into Healing Seed II. Now restores 2hp per second for 10
seconds and another 10hp upon expiration.
Congratulations! You have gained rank 7 in Healing Seed II.

I didn't even have to consider where to put my new attribute points. We needed to get beyond the barrier. I placed them in Constitution. I wished it mattered more. Each point in a base attribute beyond 10 only earned me a 1% increase. Without my Mark of the Slave debuff, I would have had a 4% increase instead of 1%. The system was odd like that. The real power in this realm wasn't in attributes. It was in skill and gear and magic. The creators made it that way for a reason. A level 1 player with good gear would always be able to beat a level 20 player with no skills, armor, or weapons. And leveling skills required challenge, more challenge than Clifford was currently offering me by killing rats in a cave.

Secret name: Slanaitheoir (savior)

Character name: Michael Dian-Cecht

Race: Dark Elf

Age: 27

Class: Undefined

Talent: Undefined

Level 4 (301xp to next level)

Health: 152 (132)

Mana: 150 (130)

Stamina: 132

Fatigue: 93%

Armor: 37 (.5% damage mitigation) - 1.3% damage mitigation with skills.

Strength: 9 (12-3)

Intelligence: 10 (13-3)

Wisdom: 10 (13-3)

Constitution: 11 (14-3)

Agility: 10 (12-3)

Luck: 2 (5-3)

Alignment: Chaotic Good (+1)

Racial Traits: +5% to herbalism, +5% to nature-based healing and damage spells, +5% to mana regeneration

Profession: Undefined

Company: Undefined

Modifiers: Mark of the Slave (-3 to all attributes), +10% movement speed, Dark Elf (-10% damage/healing during the day, +10% damage/healing at night or in dark places)

Skills:

Novice Blades 1 (.25% increase damage)

Novice Staves 5 (1.5% increased damage, 2% increased chance to block)

Novice Grappling 1 (1% increase damage)

Novice Light Armor 4

Novice Observation 6

Novice Stalking 6
Novice Tailoring 1
Novice Tracking 1
Novice Leadership 5
Novice Herbalism 1

Spells:
Novice Healing Seed II (rank 7)

9

"Here's where things get interesting," Clifford said as we left the tunnel to enter a constructed chamber. The room was more like a dungeon, with thick stones on the floor, walls, and ceiling. There was a large wooden door opposite us surrounded by four different pillars, each containing a different etching.

"This place was designed to offer unique challenges based on party roles. I've gone through them all multiple times with friends and family. Take a look and pick what you want."

I stepped into the room with great care. Examining the first pillar, I ran my fingers across an impression of a shield.

The next section of this dungeon will be attuned to the tanking role. Rewards will be more useable for tanks. Do you wish to proceed?

I dismissed the prompt and moved onto the second and third pillars. One was for ranged damage and the other for melee. The last pillar had a green leaf engraved into the mossy stone.

The next section of this dungeon will be attuned to the healing role. Rewards will be more useful for healers. Do you wish to proceed?

RJ CASTIGLIONE

"Jackpot." Selecting the healing pillar caused the room to rumble. Dust fell from the ceiling into my eyes. The giant door in the back of the chamber shifted on its hinges, swinging open to reveal a brightly lit chamber full of lush plants, trees, vines, and flowers. I stood in awe for a minute to admire the scenery. It had only been a few weeks, but seeing even the illusion of daylight filled me with warmth. I hadn't realized the amount of hope and comfort daylight brought.

"That doesn't look so bad," I said to Clifford as I stepped into the doorway. He yelled for me to wait but was too late. The doors slammed shut, and the room began to shake. I launched backward and crashed into Clifford's chest.

Wrapping his arm around me, he pulled me around his body, placing himself in front of with his shield and sword at the ready. I admired his strength, and felt comfortable with him, as though we had known one another for our entire lives. I could sense him becoming intimate with me, and I welcomed it.

Half of the torches in the room were extinguished, filling the chamber with a chill I hadn't noticed before. A hissing noise reverberated through the room. An outline of a shadow appeared on the door. I thought my eyes were playing tricks on me, but no amount of blinking prepared me for what would happen next.

The black mass peeled itself off of the wall and joined us in three dimensions. The chill penetrated deeper. My sweat was freezing to my skin. The cold penetrated my muscles and infused itself with my bones.

Creature: Jefat
Creature Type: Dark Spirit
Level: 11
Health: 225
Mana: 215

"What is that thing?"
"It's your challenge." Clifford was clanking his sword and shield together to draw the creature's attention.
"My challenge? My challenge is behind the door!" I had already

started shivering from the cold and saw my health slowly declining 1 point every few seconds.

"Your challenge IS the door. You have to," Clifford was cut off when the creature attacked, swinging its broad arms into a bear hug. He caught one arm with his shield and ducked below the other.

"Michael! Do something! You have to figure it out!"

With my health still declining, down 5 points already, I cast healing seed on Clifford and myself. The green tendrils of the spell enveloped our breastbones before dissolving into our bodies. I felt the mana cost of the spells cloud my mind, causing me to shuffle backward. Catch my balance, I picked up my staff, sidestepped Clifford and struck the creature's torso. The enchantment triggered but caused the creature no damage or push back. It had completely resisted my attack.

For good measure, I tried to attack it with my dagger with the same result. It was immune to damage.

"What are you doing? This is a healer challenge!" Clifford yelled above the sound of the now shrieking shadow. His health had dropped to 550/674. I would cast Healing Seed, but my puny spell wasn't enough to heal him to full. He wasn't about to die.

Stepping back from the creature, I recalled the last boss I had battled. The golem couldn't be killed by attacking it alone. It had to run out of mana. This creature enjoyed a similar defense: near immunity to damage. I cast healing seed on the black mass. It worked. The monster's health began to decline, first by 2 health per second for ten seconds, blooming for 7hp. This wasn't going to be enough. I couldn't keep us alive, wait for my mana to regenerate, and kill the creature with kindness. But I had a little trick that Clifford didn't know about. Raising both hands towards the creature, I chanted words of power, directing my mana into both hands instead of one. The strain of my first dual-cast triggered a cold sweat. My hands were trembling in resistance.

Before my casting completed, I infused mana into the spell, enough to cover the dual-cast and then some. Despite my new body's inexperience, knowledge trumped skill. The spell ignited in my hands—five green tendrils lashing out and honing in on the jefat, penetrating its torso in healing splendor. The drain left me wrecked, but functional.

New notifications blinked in the corner of my eye just waiting to be read.

Lunacy was the only word to describe what happened next. A shrill scream shook the room, knocking me out of my mental stupor. The jefat stopped attacking Clifford to break across the chamber. If it ever had a mission in life, it was to end mine. I sprinted away from the monster and ran laps around the room like a cat with its tail on fire, screaming all the way like a madman.

I brought up the jefat's health bar. Clifford was chasing after it, poking the shadow in a vain attempt earn back its attention. That wasn't going to happen. The spell was stronger than I realized. Each healing pulse brought down its health by 15hp. Both the seconds and my stamina slipped away.

The entire chamber seemed frozen in a slow motion caused by my own anticipation. When the ten seconds had expired, I slowed down to wait for the glorious explosion of natural healing magic. The creature only had 48 health left. I was rewarded when the green tendrils rushed out of the creature and encompassed its body for one final and glorious pulse. At this point, it looked more like a tree than a shadow monster. 52 beautiful healing points brought it to the ground, sliding across the floor in a broken heap. The jefat let out one final wail before fading to dust.

With a beaming grin on my face, I stopped running. I collapsed into a column, sucking in air like an asthmatic in a cigar lounge.

"So." Gasp. "How." Gasp. "Did I." Gasp. "Do?"

Clifford was hunched over with his hands propped on his knees for support.

"How did you do-" He was angry. "How did you do that? What did you do! In all my life. I've never-"

He raised his fists in frustration towards me, less angry now. Instead, he was flabbergasted.

"What does your little monkey think of your fireworks display?"

"Lemur. And I can't tell. He's rolling around laughing his ass off."

We reviewed the fight for two more minutes, Clifford still perplexed by my ability to transform a spell on the fly. I understood why he was dumbfounded. No person in Fjorygn could enjoy the "deus ex machina" knowledge I possessed in this realm. I may have only been level 4, but I had the insight and knowledge of someone far more advanced. I still couldn't cast my old spells, though. I still had to learn those the hard way. I was just pleased spell augmentations still worked.

We rested for a few minutes to give ourselves a chance to recuperate. I cast healing seed a few more times to bring Clifford and me back to full health. It was easier for me with my mutant healing boost. Clifford had to wait for his gashes to close and his bruises to fade with only a touch of low-level healing magic. We both had to wait for our fatigue to diminish. That required rest, food, and water. I took the chance to review my notifications:

You are afflicted with death freeze. The presence of a jefat reduces your health by 1hp every 5 seconds.
The jefat has resisted your staff attack.
The jefat has resisted your staff enchantment.
The jefat has resisted your dagger strike.
Congratulations! You have discovered a new skill. Dual-casting (current rank 1). You may weave two spells into one for 2.5x the normal mana rate. This can backfire causing damage and a waste of mana. Spells of the same type will be 3x more effective. Spells of varying types will yield different results. Increase in rank to reduce the chance of spell backlash.
Congratulations! You have discovered a new skill. Mana infusion (current rank 1). You may pour a percentage of your mana into a spell, amplifying its effects. At your current rank, you must use all remaining mana. Increase in rank to gain more control over how much mana you expel.
Congratulations! You have gained rank 9 in Healing Seed II.
You have killed a level 11 jefat. Bonus for creature over six levels above you. +177xp
You have completed the quest: "Errands, Errands everywhere!"
Reward: +145xp and disposition increase with Clifford Grey II
Congratulations! You have reached level 5! You have 2 attribute points to assign. 511xp to next level.

I did my little leveling dance as I committed my two free attribute points to Constitution. Clifford and Vindur were not impressed with my moves. Now rested, the two of us continued. The giant doors opened once again to reveal the beautiful garden within. I looked at Clifford with trepidation in my eyes. With a smug huff, he pushed me forward into the next chamber.

The aroma of flowers filled my nostrils. It smelled like the inner ring of Elatha; only with more variety and sunlight. Wherever we were, we appeared to be beyond the barrier. My companion explained to me that it was outside of Elatha, but the vertical exits to the chamber were sealed by a powerful barrier spell well beyond any of our capabilities to dispel.

Dismayed by his answer, we continued into the room, following a footpath for a few minutes. He had his weapons stored. It was a sign that there were no remaining enemies in this dungeon.

"So that's it? Rats and a shadow creature?"

"What did you expect? This place was tamed ages ago. The only reason the creatures remain is for fodder. Parents bring their kids here to practice their skills. The tank room was always my favorite. It has a rock monster that can only be killed by pushing it off a cliff. The melee and range fighting rooms are more or less the same: an onslaught of goblins either close-up or at a distance."

He continued to explain the merits of each fight and the skills that were raised by them. I failed to care the moment I saw my prize: a glistening chest in a pool of water so still and clear that it could have been a mirror into another world.

We jumped across a path of stones in the pond like children playing hop-scotch. The small island smelled like freshly cut grass. It was pillowy and soft, almost swallowing the chest completely. Almost. I popped it open to examine the contents within. Among a few minor healing and mana potions, each restoring 30 health or mana, it contained a pouch with three gold. At the bottom of the chest, the loot screamed to me:

Herb pouch: a ten slot pouch that fits within your inventory for the storage of herbs. The pouch does not occupy an inventory spot.

Ring of Lesser Magical Insight. Quality: Good. Class: Uncommon.
+25mp.
Necklace of Healer's Might. Quality: Good. Class: Uncommon.
Increases healing and damage of all spells by 1%.
Spell Tome: Nature's Grace I. This spell infuses the wounds of your
target, healing for 3hp per second for 4 seconds. Mana cost: 10.
Cast time: 1 second.
Level requirement: 7

I immediately placed the ring on my finger and the necklace around my neck. While disappointed at not being able to use the spell tome, I was happy to have my second healing spell. It was more appropriate for spot-healing my allies. Healing Seed was great but slow. You couldn't often wait for the bloom.

"Proud of your new trinkets? I thought you would be." Clifford was laying on the grass looking up at the sun. I closed the chest and took my place next to him.

"Thank you for bringing me here. It really made a difference."

"I thought it might. I still have questions. Like how you managed to kill that creature without my having to cast a single healing spell. Or how you gained two levels in less than a few hours. I've taken my cousins through here many times. It takes up to ten trips for them to even gain one level."

I turned my head to speak to him. Our eyes locked. I tried to form the words to tell him, but know Mannana's curse would prevent me. I just shrugged and broke our gaze.

"I want to tell you. I do. And I will. When the time is right, you can know everything there is to know about me."

"Well. Let's start with something simple for now, assuming you can answer. What does your last name mean?"

I smiled at him and sat up, brushing grass from my pants and shirt. Whispering a word of power, I cast healing seed on him, the drain of mana blurring my vision. "Healer. It means healer."

He punched me gently in the shoulder, an expression of blossoming friendship.

"And now I have a question. This place is called Nott's Sanctum. So. Where is Nott?"

Clifford's calm demeanor changed to fear when I said the name of the lord of the dungeon. He shot to his feet and backed away from me.

"You shouldn't have said his name! I forgot to warn you! He hates his name! Run!" He had to yell over the resonating roar that filled the chamber.

The cavern began to boom and tremble. Clifford pushed me toward the water, and we skipped across the stone path with as much haste as we could muster. Rocks began to fall from the ceiling in front of and behind us.

"Run! Keep moving!" It didn't help. The size of the debris grew larger and larger—razor-sharp stalactite's intent on joining their brother stalagmites. Clifford had already run in front of me, dragging me behind him by my hand. We were almost to the entrance of the cave, but were too late. A large crack echoed across the room, and a boulder the size of a dog fell from the roof, heading right for Clifford. He looked up, frozen in fear. A bestial roar exploded from my throat when I lunged for him. I pushed him out of the way, too late to avoid the incoming deluge of rock and stone. I was only able to say one thing before the boulder crushed my skull. "One week."

Damage received: 1847.

You have been killed. You will resurrect at Grey Estate in one week.

Congratulations! Your self-sacrifice has earned eternal respect from your surviving comrade! Your relationship with Clifford Grey II has increased from Trusted to Ally. He will follow you anywhere so long as you remain in good standing. Aside from death. He will not follow you here.

Standing over my real body was a new experience for me. It happened when I played the game, but it was never really my body. It was my avatar. This time was for real. Clifford was yelling now, tears forming in his eyes. I could tell he was screaming my name, but it sounded distant and far away, as though he were underwater.

The rocks around us had stopped falling. Nott was apparently an asshole, placated enough by my death as a fitting punishment for saying his name. I made a mental note to get stronger, come back, and bash his head in with a rock. I was dismayed when a quest alert didn't appear.

The once lush and green chamber was now cloudy, cloaked in a brilliant silver-blue light, the haze of the spirit world. I knelt beside my body, watching Clifford now gripping my corpse in his arms. He was inconsolable, water pouring from his eyes. The tears softened his square features. He had stopped screaming, now resigned to his grief at losing his new friend.

I felt a tug at my pant leg. Vindur had managed to cross over with me. He was sitting next to me, sorrow in his eyes.

"I died."

"I know."

"It didn't hurt."

The lemur didn't respond. I lifted my hand and tried to place it on Clifford's head. It passed right through him. I didn't know what I had expected. I've been in this spirit world before. Many times. Only I never had to wait a full week to resurrect. It usually only took a minute.

"What should I do for a week?"

"Whatever you want. You can't wander too far. You can only go one-hundred feet from here or your resurrection point at any time."

This was a concept I was familiar with. While I could will myself back and forth between my death-site and the nearest graveyard, I could go no further. Usually, I waited around to be resurrected. But then I suppose there was no resurrection in the real Fjorgyn.

Clifford collected my body and my possessions, slinging my light corpse over his shoulders. This was one benefit of being only five feet tall. I followed him as he walked the slow line back to the entrance of the cave, but could go no further than fifty feet beyond the trial chamber. I hit an invisible barrier. My only choice was to watch my friend disappear into the fog.

I didn't want to stay there. Not only because it was lonely and desolate; it was also home to a powerful being who I had pissed off with a single word. I willed myself back to the estate. The world around me vanished into darkness. Wind encircled me as though I were in the eye of a tornado. Moments later, I was standing in the fountain outside of Clifford's estate. The silver fog took on a darker hue there, casting the entire spirit realm in a purple haze.

I could hear the muffled voices of others nearby—my friends going about their preparations for our great escape, oblivious to my demise. A handful of guards were patrolling the perimeter of the estate. Neeta and Junta were running around, Neeta holding up the hem of her dress, holding a giant bushel of freshly picked herbs. Their laughing was muffled, a faint echo of the world I was now removed from.

I continued to observe them. Neeta would spin in circles while Junta would run off, pick some herbs, and run back in a perpetual game of fetch.

"The first thing I'll have to do when I resurrect is to start on those potions," I said to Vindur. The lemur had already settled on my shoulder, his ringed tail wrapping around my neck like a boa constrictor. His body was rigid with tension. He didn't want to be there. And I didn't want to send him away.

Hours had passed. The spirit world grew darker. More specifically, the sun had set leaving the barrier around Elatha without its daytime opaqueness.

The gates to the estate slowly creaked open, revealing a despondent Clifford still carrying my body. Once inside, he set me down at the foot of the fountain. I crouched down to get a closer look at him. I had only known the man for a few weeks, yet his face told the story of one who had lost a dear friend. His eyes were bloodshot and puffy. My blood had soaked his armor and undershirt. His despair made sense. Relationships in Fjorgyn functioned differently compared to Earth. On Fjorgyn, they were driven more by disposition. One couldn't help lament the death of a trusted ally. On earth, friends were often forged out of mutual convenience. I doubted my friends mourned my death. My company would offer grief counseling, for sure. No one would go. My family would be anguished. I mulled over my dire thoughts. They would have a wake and a funeral. Everyone would come. At the post-funeral gathering, people would eat cold food, drink alcohol, and talk about experiences they shared with me, Michael Semione. A few would stand in the corner; those who were compelled to come but never really knew a damn thing about me.

Now I was crying. Not because of Clifford or my multiple deaths. I missed my family. I missed my mother and father. They were always loving, kind, and supportive. They broke themselves in life to make sure my sisters and I wanted for nothing, treating me with a particular care as both the baby of the family and the only son. I missed my middle sister. We were always close. Even when we went to college, I chose a school in the same city as her. And I missed my oldest sister, too. She and I were not as close, but I loved her all the same. It was the beginning of autumn when I died. I was glad for that. The fall was always my favorite time of year. The energy of the summer would fade, and pool parties would be replaced with evening bonfires and hot apple cider.

By this point, the guards had helped their master carry my body behind the estate. I tried to follow only to hit the edge of the fog around me. It was too far. I chose instead to settle down by the fountain, remaining there with Vindur trembling on my shoulder, drifting in and out of a numb and empty meditative state, broken periodically by echoes of my friends and their despair. I didn't hear Neeta cry. I was grateful for this. Perhaps she was too young to understand what happened. Or maybe she cried in silence.

Hours passed. The crying had ceased. The lights dimmed in the estate. The only exception was the light to Clifford's bedroom. It shone through the darkness and death-haze like a lighthouse on a rocky shore during a midnight storm.

Words escaped me after I willed myself into his room. Half the room was blocked by the dense fog of my the spirit shroud. The other half revealed Clifford collapsed into a deep sleep. The path from his door to his bed was strewn with discarded clothes and muddy tracks. He lay fully disrobed on his sheets, now soiled with dirt and blood. His face was buried in a pillow. Others would have been embarrassed or ashamed to catch him in such a state: dirty with his ass exposed. I didn't care. I knelt beside his bed, resting my chin on his padded sheets, my face a foot from his. I saw guilt and sadness mirrored back at me.

I couldn't help but admire the man. He was the most interesting person I had met. I realized that he could become my best friend or, perhaps, something even more. It was all there. The physical contact, the locked eyes, the smirking. I wanted to return the feelings, and I didn't want to wait a week to do it.

"Vindur, can you show yourself to him? Can you tell him I'm fine?"

The lemur shook his head. He could control who saw him, but only in the realm I currently occupied.

"I'll make it up to him, then. He'll understand. My temporary death is a small price to pay for his life."

I knelt by his bed for hours hoping my presence would somehow offer him comfort. It didn't. He woke up with a start multiple times only to fall into a fitful sleep again. When that happened, I could see the blood pulsing in the veins in his neck, exacerbated by the entire ordeal. He woke up one final time, looking both at me and through me. Abandoning sleep, Clifford dragged himself out of bed, wrapped a sheet around himself and left the room where I couldn't follow.

10

"I can't do it, Vindur! I can't take it anymore. I'm going insane!"

"Perhaps you can meditate again?"

"No. I've been meditating all week. It doesn't help. I need to… I need to do something!"

I had resigned myself to walking laps around the fountain having spent the entire week so far observing others. Guards would rotate their shifts. Neeta and Junta would gather herbs. Junta was still running around and laughing like before. His sister, however, stood there in silence, perhaps upset that I wasn't around.

I was glad to see that deliveries had arrived: herbs and vials for potion making. They hadn't lost hope. They wanted to continue with the plan.

Some other masters came to talk to Clifford. I had hoped they were on our side. A few of them left their slaves with him. Baridorne came a few times to collect the deliveries. I saw no sign of Moga, Cilden, or Rose.

I spent nights exploring the rooms of the estate within reach. The library was available. I read whatever books Clifford left open. I could not turn the pages, so it didn't take long. The lower level dining room and lounge were often empty. The only constant companionship aside from Vindur was a sleeping Clifford. As the days crawled by, his sleep became more restful. His earlier grief had faded into a general morose. When he was awake, he was gloomy. When he was asleep, he was gloomy and nude, his preferred method of sleeping.

I was at last on my final day of time-out. I insulted Mannana under my breath for his torturous curse. A few times throughout the week I had begged Balama for release. There was never an answer. And so I meditated. And paced. And watched Neeta and Clifford. And paced. And meditated. And paced some more. I also learned that I could calm myself down by massaging the tips of my new elf ears. All the while, Vindur sat on the edge of the fountain, still as a statue. I saw him develop a faint smile after my last lap around the fountain.

"Well? What is it?"

The lemur didn't respond, although his small round ears did seem to twitch ever so slightly.

"Why can't you do something? Can't you get me out of th–"

Before I could finish the sentence, the silver/purple light of the spirit realm began to close in on me. The shroud surrounding me shrunk like a balloon having its air expelled. I thrashed at the encroaching barrier in a futile attempt to push it off. That didn't stop it from encasing me and forming to my body. It was soft at first, then hardened into a translucent carapace. When it couldn't mold around me anymore, it began to vibrate. The shaking penetrated my entire body. I closed my eyes to block the feeling that they would shake out of my skull. The vibrating stopped, leaving me encased in my crystal prison. When I was just about to abandon hope, I heard a loud crack, like a giant tree split in two. The world went dark and then became bright again. I found myself standing in front of the fountain with the silver light gone. Only the dark and purple haze remained. And I was naked. Again. What was wrong with this world? Why did it eat clothing like a dryer ate socks?

"Fuck you, Mannana! You perverted bastard!" I was so pleased with cursing the god of death that I hadn't taken stock of my rebirth. The spirit realm had retreated. It ejected me back into the living world. I could once again see behind the house. I could see the trees over the front wall. And I saw my friends standing in the doorway to the estate with their mouths agape.

"Uncle Mike!" Neeta stepped out from behind her mother in an unsuccessful attempt to celebrate my return. Rose had grabbed her shoulders and pulled her back.

At this point, Clifford had circled the fountain, sword at the ready. "Who are you, demon?"

With one hand protecting my modesty and the other raised in defense, I backed away from Clifford. "It's me! I'm Michael. I'm your frie–"

"My friend died! Saving my life! I carried him back. We buried him! You are not him."

By this point, Cilden had mirrored Clifford, circling the opposite end of the fountain to trap me. The guards at the gate had also drawn their swords. There was only one thing I could do. I wasn't about to let them skewer me again and earn another week trapped in spiritual detention.

"Vindur, can you?"

The lemur made himself known to Clifford. The site of him was enough for my friend. He threw his sword to the side letting it clink and skid across the cobblestone plaza. He lunged at me and caught me in the strongest bear hug I had felt in any of my lifetimes, more forceful and enveloping than even Baridorne's.

"Clifford," I coughed. "I can't breathe."

The man was overjoyed, lifting me off my feet and spinning me around in unabated celebration.

"It is you!" He motioned to the others. "It's alright. It's him!"

On earth, most cultures have protocols for nudity and personal space. This cultural trait did not exist in Fjorgyn. Cilden and Rose both offered me a welcoming embrace. Neeta had sat on my foot and clutched my leg, tears flowing down her little face in ecstatic abandon. When they had let me go, Baridorne clapped me on the back leaving a giant, red handprint on my skin. Even Moga, the coldest among us, wore a smile, although that didn't prevent him from lazily leaning against the alabaster pillar at the front door.

When they were done rejoicing my return, they gave me some

room. I stood there with my cheeks on fire and my hands cupping my manhood.

"I am thrilled to be back. I'd be more thrilled with some clothes, though." They all laughed at me, making jokes about having 'seen it all before.' Cilden had to pry Neeta from my leg to allow Clifford to lead me into the house.

He brought me into his bedroom. I had never been there before—at least not while I was alive. Closing the door, he turned to me, wearing both kindness and confusion on his face.

"Now you owe me some answers. First, let's start with what this is all about," he said as he shook his hand through my hair.

He walked me over to a mirror next to his bed, leaving me for a moment to search the contents of a nearby wardrobe.

Looking in the mirror, I saw my now apparent transformation. I couldn't help but think about how much I have changed in the last month. I woke up from death as a human in my old earth body. I then endured a magical plastic surgery so severe it would make Michael Jackson jealous. My skin had gone from tan to gray and now to a plain white. My hair had gone from a vibrant and glowing brown to a dull tan to its current silver blue. It wasn't all bad. When I had woken up, I was as soft as a baby. Although I was still squishy, my hands were now calloused; my muscles were more toned. I even felt taller. I brought up my notifications:

> *Know this! You have spent an extended amount of time in the spirit world. Your race has been modified from 'Dark Elf' to 'Spirit Elf'. You are now more in tune with the spiritual and magical energies of the world. +10% to all damage and healing done. -10% to all magical damage taken. +10% increase to all physical damage taken.*
>
> *Congratulations! You have learned a new spell! Spirit Trek. Once per week, you may summon a portal to bring you and your party from your current location to your resurrection site. You are currently bound to resurrect at the estate of Clifford Grey II. This is a fixed ability and cannot increase in skill. This is a permanent ability. You cannot lose it when changing races.*

Interface
Secret name: Slanaitheoir (savior)
Character name: Michael Dian-Cecht
Race: Spirit Elf
Age: 27
Class: Undefined
Talent: Undefined
Level 5 (511xp to next level)
Health: 148
Mana: 144
Stamina: 148
Fatigue: 0%
Armor: -10 (you're naked, jackass)
Strength: 12
Intelligence: 13
Wisdom: 13
Constitution: 16
Agility: 12
Luck: 5
Alignment: Chaotic Good (+1)
Racial Traits: +5% to herbalism, +5% to nature-based healing and
*   damage spells, +5% to mana regeneration*
Profession: Undefined
Company: Undefined
Modifiers: +10% movement speed, Spirit Elf (+10% to all damage and
*   healing done. -10% to all magical damage taken. +10% increase*
*   to all physical damage taken)*

I was so fixated on my physical appearance that I hadn't noticed my collar was gone. Although it was forced on me for only three weeks, I could still feel the itch of it on my neck, the rough leather of it scratching and chafing of my skin. I swiped my fingers across my neck where the collar had once been, sliding them down my trapezius and deltoid until I felt the rough and scarred skin of the slave brand.

"I know what you're thinking." Vindur broke the silence, now visible to only me again. "It's a magical mark. It will remain with you so long as the magic remains intact. Once the magic is spent, you can resurrect again, and it will be gone."

"I know. If you don't mind, I'd rather not die just to erase it. The mark is a part of me now. It is a part of my experience here. Everyone else will have to keep the scars for the rest of their lives. I would like to as well."

I made a promise that day to be more careful and to never put myself in a situation where all of my friends wouldn't come out alive. I knew it was a fool's promise. But like my brand, it was one I wanted to keep.

Clifford had finished with his search and walked back across the room, his hands carrying a bundle of my possessions. He sat on the bed and offered them to me.

Staff of Force Push. Quality: Professional. Class: Rare. Damage: 17-23 DPS. Can be broken by stronger weapons. Stats: +30 MP, Sends shockwave upon striking target to push enemies back. Can disrupt spellcasting. Charges: 72/100.

Homespun Cotton Shirt. Quality: Good. Class: Common. Armor: Light(2). Can be destroyed by weapons.

Rough Leather Chest piece. Quality: Good. Class: Uncommon. Armor: Light(15). Stats: +10 HP

Homespun Pants. Quality: Good. Class: Uncommon. Armor: Light(10). Stats: +20 MP

Leather boots. Quality: Good. Class: Uncommon. Armor: Light(5). Stats: +10% movement speed

Leather bracers. Quality: Good. Class: Uncommon. Armor: Light(5). Stats: +10 HP

Ring of Lesser Magical Insight. Quality: Good. Class: Uncommon. +25mp.

Necklace of Healer's Might. Quality: Good. Class: Uncommon. Increases healing and damage of all spells by 1%.

Slave collar (broken): Mark of the Slave, -3 to all attributes. Cannot be broken by common means.

I was glad to have it all back. Even more, Rose and Clifford had apparently washed and mended my clothing. They were good as new. And I was glad to have clothes again. I was tired of walking around with nothing but my inventory bag to hide my junk. I added the broken collar, staff, and armor to my inventory and slid into my pants and shirt. Putting on the ring and necklace, I took a seat next to Clifford. It was a bit strange sitting next to him. He was much taller than me. His torso was also larger and wider. Where his feet touched the floor, mine dangled off the side of the bed. Although he was not older than me, I looked the part of the child.

"I'm sorry, Michael." I could hear the hesitation in his voice. "I forgot to warn you and you died. But," he paused to wipe a tear away, "you sacrificed yourself to save me. I don't even think my father would do that. You didn't even hesitate."

"I didn't need to."

I turned to look at him and saw the familiar look of a man examining his interface. He was reading my character sheet to learn more.

"Apparently it wasn't all for nothing. I'm no longer a dark elf. Yay." I waved my hands in the air in a shallow and sarcastic expression of celebration.

"I owe you some answers, don't I?"

"You don't have to if you're not ready."

I was ready, though. Only Vindur knew my secrets and although the lemur was good and all, I wanted a human friend. I wanted someone who knew everything. I couldn't explain it. I wanted him to know the real me.

"I'm going to tell you this from start to finish. You can ask questions when I'm finished."

He nodded his consent.

"I wasn't born to this world, Clifford. I was born Michael Semione in a place called Earth." I decided to forgo the fact that his world was a video game.

"Earth isn't like here. There are no levels. There are no attributes or skills. People don't measure themselves in rank and disposition. There is only one sentient race on Earth, and I was one of them. We called ourselves human."

I went on to explain the differences between groups of humans (religion, ethnicity, nationality). I explained how we dominated the earth and created incredible scientific advances. I told him about my parents and my siblings, my work and my hobbies. I explained our art and literature. Hours had passed, and he sat there in silence, never shifting his eyes away from mine. I couldn't tell if he believed me.

"And then I died in a storm. And I woke up here one month ago. I was naked and alone in the woods. Aside from Vindur, I had nothing and no one. When I woke up, I was still Michael Semione. I was given the choice of selecting a race more appropriate for this world, and I chose the elf I am now, Michael Dian-Cecht. I also have some passive effects on my skills page that you can't see." By this point, Clifford's shoulders relaxed. His face had grown warmer.

"I received a blessing from the goddess Balama. She granted me more attributes per level, faster healing, a boost to all experience I earn, and the ability to resurrect. She also gave me immortal life." Clifford gasped a bit when I said this, but I continued. "I also received a curse from Mannana. You're familiar with him. He limited Balama's blessing. I can only receive two attribute points per level up to level until level 20. He cursed me with a one week delay between death and resurrection. He required I eat, drink, and sleep and subjected me to fatigue. He also took away the gift of immortality. I will age like you, only much slower. Most importantly, Mannana forbade me from telling anyone who was not my ally."

Clifford mulled over what I said to him. I was confident he understood. I was not sure if he accepted it.

"I have one question. You've explained most things. I know why you were such a low level. I know why you are increasing in level and skill so quickly. I even know why you resurrected. How, though, were you able to dual-cast and what did you do to make your healing spell so strong?"

I thought about his question, wanting to be careful in mentioning the game.

"People in my world invented a technology that let us transport our minds into alternate realities. Many of those realities were like yours. I spent months of my life in one such world where I learned about magic and spell casting. I've retained this knowledge."

I could tell he didn't get it. But he accepted it. The moment the last word left my mouth, we both received notifications.

You have completed the quest: "Furry Lemur and friends."
Reward: +120xp, your standing with Clifford Grey II has improved.

Clifford was smiling more than me. He was now level 18. We compared our experience gains. I learned that I was earning twenty times the amount of experience compared to him. Usually, he said, shared quests give the same amount of experience despite level.

"I'm glad we've had this talk," Clifford said. The way he was looking at me made the room feel smaller and more intimate. I had just spent the last few hours pouring my heart out to him. When I talked about my parents and sisters, I even cried. Being separated from them still broke my heart.

By the time I finished regaling him with my life's story, our backs had started to hurt. Resting back on the bed, we both lay there in a comfortable silence. I could tell Clifford wanted to say something. He was still guarded.

"What's wrong?" I asked.

He hesitated to respond, chewing on his lip to relieve anxiety and tension.

"When you saved me, I was overwhelmed with grief and guilt. I was meant to keep you safe. I brought you in there with the best of intentions. I was distracted. I forgot to warn you about Nott." Tears formed in the corners of his eyes. He turned his head away from me.

"Hey, don't be like that." I put my hand on his shoulder to comfort him, drawing his gaze back to me. "I saw you, you know. The spirit realm overlaps this one. For the entire week, I could only stay in the courtyard or the front rooms. I saw you grieve. I wanted to tell you it would be alright. I tried to when you were sleeping, but couldn't break through."

Clifford blushed a little after learning I saw him in bed. I could almost feel the heat from his cheeks from a foot away.

"If I had to go through all of this again, I wouldn't change a thing. Even if I were never to resurrect, I would have saved you. I'm a healer. That's what we–"

The tense man lunged forward, closing the space between us with warmth and moisture emanating from his body to form steam in his chilly bedroom. He gripped my head in his hands and kissed me on the lips with a fervor. For a brief moment, I was shocked. That faded when the heat of passion overwhelmed me. The room around me darkened until all that remained were his large hands and imposing torso. I was sure he could feel my heart pounding against his hands. I kissed him back. He tasted of salt and soap and honey. Although it seemed like hours had passed, it had only been a few moments. Before I lost myself to our combined passions, he slid his hand down my neck to plant his palm on my chest.

Clifford pushed himself away from me, shooting out of bed. He stood with his back facing me, looking at me only through the mirror. "I'm sorry. I shouldn't have." The man was embarrassed and dismayed at having lost control.

I reached out to him and grabbed his hand, forcing him to turn around.

"It's alright. I sensed your feelings before. And they're not unwelcome. It's just been a while for me." I pulled him back to the bed and had him lay down beside me, our heads both propped by his feather pillows. A few quills poked out and scratched my neck. "Can you just be here with me? It's been a week since I've felt anything or anyone."

The young man smiled, putting his arm around me and pulling me closer to him, my head resting on his chest. He kissed the top of my head with care and tenderness. I hadn't been this comfortable with someone before, man or woman. That is what I loved most about Fjorgyn. On Earth, many people had expectations about behavior, decorum, and proper relationships. That didn't translate here. This world was rough and full of opportunities to die. People embraced passion and love wherever they could find it.

"Michael, I don't take intimacy like this lightly. While I lost control a moment ago, I want you to know what this means to me. I believe in you. In such a short time, you have become my dearest friend. I will follow you anywhere but only if you're willing. Do you accept?"

I thought about this. When I met Clifford, I figured he was a spoiled elitist. I have never been more mistaken in my entire life. Here was a vigorous and beautiful man who, despite owning me, committed himself to freeing hundreds of slaves because I wanted to. He mourned for me not as a man who has lost a slave, but as a man who had lost a lover. What he was suggesting was not a reversal of roles. It was a commitment to an enduring bond of friendship. Would I be willing to offer him the same in return? His body tensed, waiting for a response.

I tilted my head up and planted a gentle kiss on his cheek. "I accept. We will follow one another anywhere and everywhere."

> *Congratulations! Your expression of true friendship and love has changed your relationship with Clifford Grey II. Your disposition with him has increased from Ally to Companion. Your interests and fates are now intertwined. Do not forsake your companions. Doing so comes at a great cost to you both. +150xp received.*

I was wholly content to rest in the nook he created for me, the top of my head pressed against his stubble and my face anchored against his collarbone. He smelled of jasmine and musk and earth. I fell asleep to the feeling of his hand stroking the side of my head from my temples to the point in my ear. For the first time since arriving in Fjorgyn, I slept a sleep of contentment. I dreamed of brighter days to come. And of good days with my family and friends. And of Clifford and our newfound companionship.

11

I woke up to a room filled with darkness. Of course it was dark. It was always dark. The only source of light was glowing embers in the fireplace opposite the bed. I was resting on my side, sheets wrapped around me like a tortilla encompasses a burrito. I felt Clifford's weight shift beside me; his arm draped over me as if to keep me safe. Turning to look at him was enough to draw him out of sleep. He had gotten up in the night to put me under the covers and get himself ready for bed. He slept on top of the covers with only his shirt off, although I knew that his preference to sleep was in the buff.

"Good morning," he mumbled, stretching his long arms and arching his back to push out the sleep. Was it morning? I could never tell.

"How long was I asleep?"

"Fourteen hours."

I did some quick math. It was now around 10 AM the next day. I felt a pang of guilt having slept so long. I was sure that he had to get up for food and to lock down the house for the night. Clifford made a point to check the house was secure. This prevented nosy masters from discovering what we were up to. I had also not talked to Cilden or the others. I hoped they weren't mad at me.

Clifford sat up. There was a look of ease about him. Yawning, he looked at me and quietly said one word, "Breakfast?"

I nodded and jumped out of bed, almost tripping over the sheets in the process. I had one leg planted on the ground and the other shackled by a knot in the bedsheet.

He started laughing at my predicament and helped me free my leg. With both feet now on the ground, I stood there in triumph having escaped my nasty, linen tormentor.

"But first," he said while pointing to my lower half, "you should take care of that."

I looked down with confusion only to realize why he was laughing. I was pitching a tent, the burden every man had in the morning.

"You know, you're kind of big for an elf."

I smiled at him, pushing my erection down with my hands. My cheeks were on fire when I responded, "Yeah. I got to choose what I looked like. And I decided to keep my... human anatomy".

I hesitated briefly while I slithered away from the bed, Clifford just shaking his head at me in humorous resignation. I turned away and headed for the bathroom to void myself.

His bathroom, like his bedroom, was spotless. I half-expected the room to be disgusting. He never let his slaves clean it. The entire room screamed "luxury." If I didn't know better, I would half expect to see this bedroom featured in a design magazine on Earth. The tiled floors and walls were cut into perfect rectangles. Elatha had indoor plumbing and an advanced sewer system. Heating and moving the water was both mechanical and magical. I raised my arm up and sniffed myself. Although I wasn't dirty, I smelled different. I smelled metallic—a clear consequence of being encased in ancient magic.

I turned on the faucet to the tub and stopped the drain. The water came out the perfect temperature for a bath. While it filled, I relieved myself and disrobed. Full of excitement at the prospect of my first hot bath since my arrival in Fjorgyn, I rushed into the water, completely submerging myself in its wonderful warmth. The heat of it penetrated deep into my body, caressing my very bones.

When I came up for air, Clifford was standing in the doorway. Before I could motion for him to join me, he discarded his clothes and jumped into the oversized tub. It could have easily fit three more people. Or Baridorne. I was not about to call him up there, though.

We splashed around and cleaned ourselves for another thirty minutes before the water started to lose its warmth. Before shrinkage set in and our fingers pruned beyond repair, we escaped the water and wrapped towels around our waists, returning to his bedroom with our clothes in hand.

The bedroom was warmer. Clifford had added more wood to and stoked the fire. The light of it danced across the walls casting mystical lights and shadows. With the warmth of the bath still enveloping our bodies, we both put our clothes on and got ready for the day. I stood in the mirror for far too long to arrange my silver hair. Clifford had also put out a plate of bread, cheese, and fruits for our breakfast. I stuffed my face with the food while he looked on in bemusement.

"What? I haven't eaten in a week," I said, my cheeks packed with grapes and bread.

By the time we had finished everything, it was already 11 AM. I had to start the day. I had so much work to catch up on if we were going to plan our escape. Pleased and in high spirits from my evening and morning long retreat from the world, I motioned for us to leave the room.

"Are you forgetting something?" he asked while pointing to his neck.

"It's broken." I knew I had to wear my collar but resisted putting it back on.

Clifford pulled a new collar out of his inventory and handed it to me. It was different. It was softer and lighter. It also had a hidden latch in a seam so it could be removed with ease if one knew how.

"Last week, I removed everyone's collar and offered these replicas. Some of the other masters are doing the same. The new ones will fool any master or guard. None of them look at slaves long enough to notice the difference."

I nodded my consent, allowing him to slip the collar around my neck, showing me how the latch worked. When he finished, he offered me a soft kiss and ushered me out of the room, closing the door behind me with a promise to see me later. When I heard the door latch shut, I was dismayed. The previous evening and this morning were perfect. I had nearly forgotten about the tasks at hand and my prior death. And for the first time in a month, I didn't have nightmares. I didn't wake up missing my old life. Shaking the negative feelings from my mind, I went looking for the others. I also had to find Vindur. I hadn't seen him since my resurrection.

As I walked into the basement, a miasma of dried herbs punched me in the face. It smelled like my grandmother's house. The bedrooms and the washroom were all empty, but the kitchen and lounge were as busy as ever. In the last week, the group had managed to install an apothecary cabinet. Each drawer was labeled with herbs that were prepared and ready for use. The remaining ingredients were hanging in bundles on the wall waiting to be dried.

Rose was leaning over a pot, shaking her head in frustration. I could smell the herbs burning at the bottom of the container. I startled her with a cough, my attempt to vacate from my lungs the vile concoction.

"What are you making? It's awful!"

She waved a wooden spoon at me. "I'm trying to make your healing potions, you ungrateful little elf!" She glared at me. I glared at her. Before long, laughter exploded from our lips. Rose dropped the spoon and met me in the middle of the room, embracing me in a kind (and clothed) hug.

"I'd ask you where you've been, but I can see from your glow that you didn't spend last night alone. Neeta's been looking for you."

Rose and I spent a few minutes pouring over what they accomplished last week. The root cellar was filled to the brim with all of the herbs we needed. Clifford had sourced them from a few dozen vendor markets scattered about the city to avoid drawing unwanted attention. He procured all the vials we need from his friends. Neeta and Junta spent their days gathering more herbs from the estate gardens. They had both gained two levels and committed their new attribute points to Constitution as instructed. Neeta had objected. She wanted to be wise, like her mother. Baridorne, Cilden, and Moga had all been granted permission to run Nott's sanctum with other slaves. They ran it multiple times a day, instructed by Clifford to avoid the healing branch. In the prior week, they had each gained two levels as well.

"And what about you? Why aren't you increasing your level?"

Rose frowned at me. "I'm trying, but I can't make a potion. I tried to remember your recipe. Every time I make it, the pot boils over and the herbs burn to a crisp."

She sighed, having lost more confidence in our plan. It was impossible without the healing and invisibility potions.

"Anyhow," she continued, "it doesn't matter much." She held up two uncommon class rings that offered +30HP a piece. "If I wear these, I should have no trouble with the barrier. I can then throw them back to others to wear. They're not soulbound!"

"Rose, that's brilliant." It surely was. I hadn't thought that the health boost could come from gear as well. Having enchanted gear made the plan much more likely to succeed. Only, not without the invisibility potions.

I strolled over to the cauldron hanging over the fire and analyzed the liquid. I gagged after spooning a little into my mouth.

"There are about five things wrong with what you're doing," I said.

She joined me at my side, intertwining my arm and hers as though I was escorting her to a grand ball. She glanced at the pot, then to me, then back to the pot, then to me again. I let out a sigh and did my best to avoid laughing at her.

"First, you used dried jasmine. It needs to be fresh. Second, the water is way too hot. You need to keep it at a low simmer, watching it regularly to make sure it doesn't become too hot or cold. Third, I said to make a tea, not bath water. There's way too much water here."

I stirred the contents of the pot with my finger. It scalded my skin a little. Yanking it out, I tasted the mixture again. "Fourth, and this is my mistake. You've used ground water. While that does meet the definition of fresh, it is also laced with minerals that change the solution. You need to use free-flowing water, perhaps from the canal running behind the house. Fifth, you can't start out with a higher level healing potion. You need to increase your Herbalism skill to at least rank 30 to be able to make an this potion successfully. Even then, it will fail nine times out of 10, destroying the ingredients in the process. The rate of success and potency of the drink is determined only by the maker's skill."

I turned to face her and grabbed the wooden spoon from her hand and broke it in half. "And last. Wood and bark are ingredients in many recipes. You can't make potions with a wooden spoon. It must be metal or stone."

Her face turned bright red. I couldn't help myself and started laughing at her response. My reaction earned me a slap on the back of my head.

"And how was I supposed to know all this? It's not my fault you went and got your skull flattened leaving me in the kitchen expecting me, a farmer's wife, to be a Master Herbalist!"

I ducked the next slap and caught her arm in my hand.

"Well, at least you're not as slow as a turtle anymore, Michael Dian-Cecht." She had calmed down enough and placed her hand against my cheek.

"It's good to have you back. Without you, this whole scheme would have fallen apart."

I accepted the gesture of friendship by placing my hand on hers. The way she held my face reminded me of when my mother used to comfort me.

"Now, tell me. How was your night with our young master? And don't spare any details. I'm surrounded by crude men and children all day. I could use some gossip to lighten the mood."

I enlightened Rose with all of the details after she promised me discretion. She responded by saying "and who would I tell that cares?" We cleaned up the kitchen and picked out more proper wood for the fire. The ash wood she had was ideal for cooking meat and heating a house. It burned too hot and produced too much smoke. I found what appeared to be some white pine wood that burned faster while producing less heat.

I formed two small fires in the hearth and anchored two pots above each, resting on a metal arm that could be moved in and out of the fire to control the amount of heat better.

I explained to her the basics of herbalism. It was less about creating simple concoctions and more about the ritual of setting up the mixture.

Everything had to be right. Only when the conditions and the intent were correct would the hidden properties of the herbs reveal themselves.

You could throw jasmine and ginseng root in a pot of hot water and make some nice tea. She looked at me like I was insane when I mentioned that this tea could be used to prevent people from getting common sicknesses while relieving stress and stomach aches.

It was the art of crushing the fresh or dry ingredients in a stone mortar and pestle a certain number of times with complete focus that mattered. This resulted in the release of the plant's mana. Each ingredient required special handling and treatment depending on the mixture being made. For a simple healing potion, we used ginseng root and jasmine flowers.

First, because the root was more wooden, it had to be crushed into a powder using a counter-clockwise motion with one's non-dominant hand. This had to be done quickly from a place of confidence. Only when brought to submission would ginseng root release its mana. Once released, you had seconds to pour it in simmering water to prevent the mana from escaping into the ground. The jasmine flower was much more delicate. It drew mana from the sun and the air, storing the mana in its petals and bud. Peeling off the green stalks and leaves, I showed Rose the proper motions: gently crush the flower with the stone mortar with your dominant hand in a clockwise motion no more than five times.

One had to pretend the mortar was as gentle as the wind, coaxing the flower into releasing its mana. Once complete, the mana lingered for up to an hour before being absorbed into the bud again.

"But why does this combination make a healing potion?" she asked.

"Sometimes it doesn't. This precise combination can be prepared in another way to make a weak poison. Ginseng root draws nutrition from the soil. It also expels toxins from the plant. Because we've added more ginseng root than jasmine, it is the dominant ingredient. It will draw injury from the body. The presence of jasmine flowers tells the ginseng to do this, providing the ginseng root with more mana to complete the task at hand."

"And the jasmine?"

"Jasmine is an innately peaceful plant. It exists to heal. If the jasmine were picked during a violent storm, however, the negative energy of the storm would, for lack of a better word, frighten the jasmine. Combining it with the ginseng would create a fear poison. By its nature, the ginseng root would seek to expel the fear into the poison's target, compelling it to flee. This is why I showed Neeta and Junta how to pick the flower. If you remove the flower gently, the jasmine is not afraid. It doesn't mind being put to a purpose."

"You talk about plants as though they're alive and sentient."

"They are. And they aren't. They don't think. They feel. Plants are like forces of nature. And nature can both heal or kill you. Any plant can be made to do the same."

Rose and I stood over our pots for another twenty minutes. I showed her how to stir her mixture, now using a metal spoon. We gently cradled the mixture in and out of the direct heat of the fire to avoid it boiling over.

"Now for the fun part!"

Taking our pots from the fire, I draped a cheesecloth over a large bowl and stood up a vial with a funnel. Pouring the water into the bowl caught the ingredients. Once complete, I bundled the cheesecloth and held it over the funnel and squeezed for dear life, separating the liquid from its base ingredients. The result was a vial filled to the brim with a pink solution.

You have created (1) Minor Healing Potion. Quality: Poor. Class:
Uncommon. When consumed, restores 5 health over 30 seconds.
+4xp

"That's it?" Rose was confounded. "Thirty minutes of work for one poor quality potion?"

"That's it. Once we filter the ingredients, the mana is spent. As we increase in skill, it will take us less time to make higher quality potions. The plants will respond to us faster. This mixture is limited, though. When our skill is high enough, I have another healing herb we can use to make stronger ones." I was glad both Rose and I were elves. Our race offered us a 5% boost in both quality and increasing in rank.

Rose and I spent the rest of the day making potions. We had made six more batches before the room became too noisy for us to focus on what we were doing. I had gained two levels in herbalism already. Rose only gained one. Neeta had returned with her herbs for the day and was tugging on my pant leg. "Uncle Mike! Uncle Mike! I reached level 3! Uncle Mike, aren't you proud of me? Uncle Mike! Come play with me!" I was struggling with squeezing my last potion out of the cheesecloth with Neeta yanking me away. Once complete, I acquiesced to her.

Tired of the noise, Rose kicked us all out of the kitchen and lounge. We were forced to run around in the garden. I taught the children how to play Superman tag. It was more fun once Cilden, Clifford, and the guards joined in, running from one end of the garden to the other to escape the children, only to be frozen in place waiting for another adult to crawl between their legs to free them. Baridorne even tried to join in, but he was too slow to escape Junta, a natural born sprinter if there ever was one. Moga perched himself against a wall with a grimace on his face.

"Moga! If you keep making that face, it's going to stay that way forever!" I yelled.

Neeta stopped dead in her tracks. "Really, Uncle Mike?" She thought I was serious, so I played along.

"That's right, Neeta! Now don't go making funny or sad faces unless you want to end up looking like our friend, Moga." I picked her up and spun her around listening to her giggle uncontrollably.

"Uncle Mike?" I stopped turning her and nodded. "Tag! You're frozen!"

She wiggled out of my arms leaving me free to strike my best Superman pose. "All the adults are frozen! All the adults are frozen! We win! We win!"

Neeta and Junta were holding hands and spinning around, dancing in a circle like they were playing "Ring Around the Rosie." Fjorgyn, although very different, still had so much in common with Earth.

The games ended when her mother stormed out of the house huffing at us all. She had been ringing the dinner bell for ten minutes. She was angry and was yelling. It went something like "the food is getting cold" and "I should send you all straight to bed!" and "Honestly. You're all children!"

She calmed down when Clifford, Cilden and I promised to clean the dishes.

"Well come on, then! Dinner's on the table."

All of us filed into the dining room made up to look like a great banquet. We were no longer just a household with a master, a handful of guards, and a gaggle of slaves. We went from ten slaves to twenty-five. Clifford sat at one end of the table. Another master, a woman, sat on his left.

Name: Nila Hislop
Race: Trisian
Age: 28
Class: Priest
Talent: None
Level: 13
Health: 321 (128)
Mana: 457 (143)
Stamina: 166 (128)
Alignment: Chaotic good (+3)
Profession: Scholar
Disposition: Indifferent
Company: Wraithheart (Junior Member)

Clifford sat me to his right and introduced me to Nila.

"So this is the slave that would free them all? I know you said he is more than he seems but Cliff," she paused to analyze and examine me, "a level 5?"

"He can dual-cast. And infuse mana into his spells. And if I'm not mistaken, he made healing potions all day with no instruction or recipe."

I held my breath hoping that Clifford wouldn't reveal the secret of my resurrection. He didn't. I felt Vindur's familiar rough fur and padded feet land on my shoulder.

"And where have you been?" I asked the lemur, anger resonating in my voice.

"Well, after you and Clifford were done frolicking this morning, I stuck around. He had a long chat with this woman when you left. I followed her."

"And what did you learn?"

"She checks out. She sold her slaves to Clifford for the average amount. She met with no one else. She went home and trained all her slaves in healing and then brought them here."

I thanked the small creature and turned my attention back to Nila.

"I'm a quick study," I said to her, forcing as much sarcasm from my voice as I could.

"I hope that's true, young elf. We're trusting you and your plan to free us all from this prison."

I squeezed Clifford's hand tightly under the table, taking my anxiety and frustration out on him. He didn't stop me. By this point, Vindur had abandoned my shoulder and was munching on some fruit he liberated from a bowl on the table. How he managed to take and eat the fruit with no one noticing was beyond me.

"Have you thought about where we would go once we're beyond the barrier?" Nila asked Clifford.

"I have an idea. About ten days south of here there's an isolated ruin in the forest. I know it well. It offers us open space, a source of food and water, and adequate shelter. It is also remote and secluded. There are no nearby Trisean cities or towns. The only nearby settlements owe no allegiance to Elatha or Levent."

I shuddered when I heard the High King's name. So did Nila. Maybe she wasn't all bad. I just had to get to know her better and improve her disposition towards me.

Clifford continued. "So will you be able to get us there? I can show you where it is on my map." White lines filled their eyes when they invoked a strange ability I had never seen before. When the lines of text faded, we sat in silence while Nila analyzed her map.

"I can get us there. I know a portal site nearby. I can go there and scout the area, setting up a closer location. I won't be able to hold it open for long. We'll have fifteen minutes to get everyone through the barrier and the portal. I suggest we escape by Nott's. It's more secluded there than at other locations. The portal will go unnoticed."

Clifford nodded his consent.

"And you, young elf." She raised her glass of wine to offer me a toast. "We're trusting you to orchestrate all of this. You came up with the plan. It's yours to execute. I wish you luck." We clanked our glasses together and emptied them. The wine rushed through my body with a vengeance. I hadn't consumed alcohol in this body before. I released Clifford's hand to better balance myself in my chair. He was laughing under his breath at the sight of my glowing cheeks and dumb smile.

We celebrated that night, masters and slaves at the same table, sharing food and wine and beer and stories. Some soon-to-be-freed-slaves danced in a line while singing songs from their childhood. When the night was nearly over, Nila said her goodbyes. I had over-imbibed and was less functional at this point, standing in the middle of the room singing Justin Timberlake's "Can't Stop the Feeling". I had introduced both shuffling and voguing to Fjorgyn. It was an instant hit. When I was done dancing and singing, Clifford and Cilden put my arms around their shoulders and carried me to my room, now deciding that we were all done for the night. I hiccuped a goodnight to Rose while she shushed me, warning me not to wake the children. Once in bed, we said our goodnight's and I dozed off for the second-best night's sleep I've had in Fjorgyn.

12

"The world is Pain. The world is Death..." I was sprawled out on the table in the kitchen, my arms extended to both sides. I planted my face on the tabletop and closed my eyes. The light from the fireplace triggered a migraine powerful enough to knock out a horse.

"You've started without me?" asked Rose, rubbing her eyes in the doorway.

"Go away!"

She ignored my demand and walked over to the hearth to smell the concoction I was brewing. "This doesn't look like any health potion you've shown me."

"It's not. Can you strain it into a cup for me?"

I propped myself up. The throbbing pain in my head jolted into my neck and shoulders. Lifting the cup, I blew gently to push the steam off the surface of the tea and took three big sips. The hot liquid ran down my throat, scalding the roof of my mouth on the way down. It was worth it. In a matter of minutes, the hydration from the tea alone helped ease my headache.

"What is it?"

"Ginger root powder made into a tea. It relieves headaches."

She took a few sips herself from the tea, cringing when the soapy bitterness of it hit her tongue.

"It's certainly something," she said, setting the cup down on the table and pushing it away.

"You can thank your husband. He dragged my scrawny ass out here and pounded the root into a powder for me. I am never drinking again!"

"Honestly, Michael, I'm surprised you were able to drink as much as you did. Most elves can only drink a glass before getting drunk. You kept up with my husband. And he can drink beer like water."

I slammed my face on the table again. I just wanted to go back to sleep. Opening one eye up, I squinted at Rose. She was leaning forward and looking down at me, her hands on her hips. She looked like my mother, ready to send me to my room for not doing my chores.

"Can you make me breakfast? Please?"

She let out a drawn out sigh but agreed none-the-less. "What do you want?"

"Eggs. And toast. And a kiwi."

"A what?"

"Nevermind. Just the eggs and toast."

"Alright. Go clean yourself up, though. You smell like a dwarf on his wedding night."

The cold water in the washroom was enough to scare away my hangover. I took the opportunity to review what we still needed to do before our escape. My plan was good, but last night made me realize I had not planned how to survive afterward. We couldn't just pop through a portal in the wilds with a few hundred people and expect to survive. We needed food and seeds. We needed weapons to hunt. We needed money to trade with nearby villages for other supplies. I also needed to gain a few more levels—this meant another trip to Nott's Sanctum. I shivered at the thought of going back into that hell-hole. Cilden and the others had gone and returned without a scratch. I was confident that as long as I didn't piss off the dungeon's master, I would be okay.

I dried myself off and dressed. I reentered the kitchen, Vindur now resting comfortably on my shoulder. Cilden and Clifford were sitting at the table inhaling their breakfast like they've never had food before. I sat down with them and ate my own, dismissing the remnants of my hangover with every bite.

"Clifford, do you think it's safe for me to reenter the Sanctum?"

He swallowed his food, surprised at my question. He must not have imagined me wanting to go back there.

"I don't see why not. Nott killed you. It's not like he took the time to learn who you are. It should be okay. Just don't say his name again."

"Moga, Baridorne and I are going. We were going to grab another healer as well. Join us," Cilden said, his mouth too full to form the words clearly.

Rose was dismayed at the prospect of losing her potions partner for the day.

"Sorry, Rose. Raincheck?"

"Rain what?"

"Nevermind. I promise that you'll have my full attention for the rest of the week. We'll be having nightmares about all the potions we're going to make. Right?"

She perked up, offering me a stout nod. She promised me that she would catch up to me in rank by the time we returned.

"Clifford, will you walk us down there? I have a few details to talk about."

"You don't have to ask."

We packed some provisions for the day: food, water flasks, and some of the potions Rose and I made.

As we left the estate, I listened to Cilden and Moga's conversation. I don't think I've heard him stitch together more than a few words before. He was obviously more comfortable with Cilden.

They reviewed the previous day's run through the sanctum. Moga had a thief's wit, making jokes about sneaking up behind his boss and stabbing him up the ass. Baridorne also walked behind them listening. It turned out he was the quiet one of the trio. After three checkpoints where we had to show our brands, we reached the edge of the city. It had taken the better part of the morning to get there, offering me enough time to review what I needed Clifford to buy for the group.

"It's a tall order, you know. Seeds and non-perishable food are heavily regulated. I'll have to call in a few favors to get enough for all of us. I can swing two months of food."

"That'll have to do. We can stretch it thin and put together a group of hunters and gatherers to find the rest. At least until we figure out our next steps."

Where the markets on the edge of town saw a significant amount of traffic, the path down to the dungeon was abandoned. A feeling of foreboding pitted itself in my stomach when we left Clifford to finish the trek to the cave's entrance. Clifford was my tank, and I was his healer. I only hope he taught Baridorne well. When we reached the wooden door, we donned our armor. The others oohed and aahed at the quality of my gear. The other healer in our group, a young level 6 Trisian, was most impressed by my staff. They were only given common class items. They each had uncommon rings on, though, earned from previous runs. My second healer was without rings.

With my armor on and my staff at the ready, I stepped into the dungeon's entrance. Just like last time, the door behind me had disappeared. To leave, we had to finish at least one challenge. "I swear to you, Cilden if I die in here I'm going to spend the next week haunting you. I mean it. If you see something attacking me, you come and rescue me."

My friend clapped me on the back hard enough to take away a health point and pressed forward. Baridorne took the lead with his shield and sword at the ready. The giant held himself like a man who had seen battle before. Cilden was behind him wielding an iron mace. Moga was next, the little Nissean sneaking along the ground with a bow in his hand. He had an arrow ready.

"Have you been in here before?" I asked the other healer. He shook his head quickly, eyes open as wide as they could responding to both darkness and tension.

"It's okay. You focus on healing Moga and me. I'll focus on you, Baridorne, and Cilden." Before I could get a response from him, Baridorne had already started clanking his sword and shield together. The first wave of rats scurried up the tunnel intent on eating their new prey. Just like last time, eight of them had appeared around the bend. I analyzed as many as I could and saw that their level had increased since I was last here, most likely in response to our higher average level. The creatures lunged forward at Baridorne. Two had already dropped dead, one by his sword and another by Moga's arrow.

Cilden managed to peel two more off of Baridorne and was swinging his mace at the creatures. He missed most of his swings, but landed one or two hits, costing one rat half of its health. At this point, both Baridorne and Cilden had taken damage. I cast healing seed on them. The second rank of the spell proved much more potent, especially when augmented by my now full wisdom. Each tick of the spell healed for 3hp. Ten seconds expired, and four more rats were dead, most by Baridorne and Moga. One had broken through, though, and jumped over Moga to attack me. These creatures weren't stupid. They knew I prevented them from enjoying their dinner.

The healer next to me screamed and cast his healing spell on me: a rank one healing prayer. It was a foolish move. I raised my staff and slammed it into the creature like a pro would swing a baseball bat. The rat took a fair amount of damage both from my staff and the wall it crashed into. This gave Moga enough time to draw his dagger and finish it off.

With the final creature dead and the party still at full health, we pressed on. I analyzed the young man while we walked.

Name: Peadair Byrne
Race: Trisian
Age: 19
Class: None
Talent: None
Level: 6
Health: 151
Mana: 152
Stamina: 151
Alignment: Undetermined
Profession: None
Disposition: Neutral
Company: None

He still had his original slave collar. I made a mental note to talk to Clifford and Nila about giving him a replica. We couldn't have our healers suffering from an Intelligence and Wisdom hit when we escaped.

"Look, Petey." I don't think he liked me playing with his name. That wasn't going to stop me. "Your only heal right now is a direct heal. If you cast it on anyone who has full health, it does nothing. The mana cost might be small. Direct heals are like that. They're slow to cast with a medium mana cost. They can also be completely wasted. There are four of us between you and the monsters. You don't have to worry. If you see Moga and I taking more than-" I paused to review my combat log. "More than 13 points of damage, then you cast it. If we're going to die, you keep casting it over and over again until we're safe or you're out of mana."

He was still tense although he nodded at me.

"You'll be okay. Don't worry. This place is easier than a walk in the park."

A smile formed in the corner of his mouth. A little reassurance went a long way in this world.

We went on like this for some time; killing rats and taking names. Petey and I cast a few healing spells. No one took more than 20 to 30 damage at any time. Moga was quick and took no damage whatsoever. We took a break in the central chamber to decide our next move. We agreed to clear each pillar one at a time to maximize experience and reward.

A hidden door slid open when we activated the tank pillar. We entered an underground cavern that was about one-hundred feet deep and thirty feet wide. Torches brightened the sides of the cave. In the distance, I heard a rumble. As Clifford promised, a large rock monster thudded towards us, moving painfully slow. Each time its foot struck the ground, the chamber shook a bit, echoes of the thud filling the room. Baridorne charged at the creature. It had begun launching rocks at us, each of us spending most of our time dodging.

Baridorne met the creature head on, slamming his shield into its torso. 10% of Baridorne's stamina vanished. With only one foot on the ground at the time, it lost its balance and stumbled ten feet back only to be met by Baridorne's shield again. Half-giant met rock monster with equal ferocity. The monster's bellows clashed with my friend's roar. It lifted its large arms and slammed into Baridorne's back, causing him to cave to his knees slightly. He maintained his footing and the creature began sliding back to the end of the cave. Cilden and Moga were picking up stray rocks and throwing it at the monster's head. Petey and I stayed back healing Baridorne every time he took a hit. Each direct heal gave him the boost he needed to push on. Each pulse of my healing seed kept his knees from hitting the ground.

The half-giant pushed like a professional football player. The edge of the cliff was only fifteen feet away. Then it was ten feet. Then it was five feet. Baridorne was almost out of stamina. I knew it would be close. Moga and Cilden might have had to finish if I didn't have my trusty staff.

Baridorne dropped to one knee having lost his balance, and the rock monster gained some ground. Before taking a full step, it's oversized head met the end of my staff. I triggered the enchant, and the creature's head launched backward taking its body with it, roaring in agony as it shattered against the rocks below.

I knelt down next to Baridorne; the gentle giant exhausted from his sumo match. Despite being three times my weight, I lifted his dead arm around my shoulder and helped him to his feet.

"Thanks. That was a bit tougher than last time."

He bent down to scoop up a small pile of loot that was on the ground where the creature had fallen: a ring granting him +2 to strength, a necklace that boosted his stamina, and a shield—the same shield he currently had.

We allowed our stamina and mana to regenerate before moving onto the melee damage challenge. A new door opened up revealing a crude underground village. Straw huts surrounded a fire pit. There was a rat roasting on a spit above the flames. Moss and slime covered the walls of the small room. On the far end of the village, there were a few holes in the wall.

"Once we step in the settlement, things might get a little crazy. We learned last time that the goblins are stupid. They won't attack you two." Cilden pointed at Petey and me. "So just don't, you know, punch any of them in the face."

The room began to rumble. Screams poured into the makeshift village from the three holes opposite us. Before I could raise my staff, roughly twenty goblins stormed into the room. They were equipped with crude stone daggers, were mostly naked, and were of low health and low level. Baridorne drew the attention of about half of the attackers. They started pounding on him. Their daggers either shattered or fell out of their hands, unable to pierce his armor. He was taking health damage, but it was nothing my healing seed couldn't handle.

Cilden and Moga had transformed completely, skirting behind the group and stabbing the creatures in the back or beating them over the head. This was the challenge for them. It took two hits per goblin to bring them down. A few turned to rage when their comrades died and began attacking anything they saw, including one another. Two had broken towards Petey and me, running in a straight line. I raised my staff and activated the enchantment. Both of them took the hit. One launched backward and slammed into the ground. The other slid a few feet back before attacking again, swinging his stone dagger in great arcs. I stumbled to the side when his dagger sliced my arm. Seeing me injured, Petey stepped forward with a knife and plunged it into the creature's stomach. Blood gushed out of the goblin, coating Petey's arm in a putrid green slime. The goblin collapsed to the ground having died from my staff strike and my new friend's courageous assault.

"Will you?" I asked him, raising my injured arm.

He took two seconds to cast the healing spell. Where Healing Seed sprouted vines that absorbed into the body, his spell was like a white poultice encompassing the wound. When the light faded, my skin was left unbroken. Only the bloodstains remained.

"A little help here, Mike!" Moga cried out, now at half health.

"Calm down, short stuff. You're fine!" He responded to my light-hearted insult with a growl.

Petey and I both cast a slew of healing spells. We looked like champions in the next few moments, brilliant white and green light illuminating our friends. When my spell finished blooming, they were all back to full health, and the last goblins were dead. Picking over their bodies, we found their rewards: two rings of health, a necklace granting +2 Agility, and an iron dagger that one goblin had on him, but hadn't used in the fight.

The third pillar room was about the same. Instead of a village in the center of the chamber, there was a giant gap dividing us from our targets, ten goblins throwing rocks and spears at us. Cilden and Moga attacked them from a distance, the Nissean with his bow and Cilden with any rock he could find to launch at them. Baridorne was laughing when rocks and spears bounced off his armor. Petey and I stood behind him to avoid the projectiles. No one was hurt.

When the room was cleared, a door opened to our right revealing a chest containing more health rings, a ring of +2 Dexterity, a ring of +2 Wisdom, a bow, and a collection of arrows.

After an hour of fighting, we were exhausted. We only had one pillar remaining. In my opinion, this was arguably the scariest and most dangerous of them all. We sat in the central chamber and had lunch: bread, cheese, and water. As we waited for our fatigue to reduce, I explained the fight to the others. I explained death freeze and told them not to worry about it. We would heal them through it. I came up with a plan that everyone understood. It involved the minor healing potions I brought with me. I distributed the nine potions I had, offering the two stronger ones from my previous run to Baridorne and the weaker ones to Moga and Cilden. Petey stood on the side of the room opposite me, and we activated the pillar.

Like last time, the door to the next chamber slammed shut. The room grew cold. The jefat emerged.

Creature: Jefat
Creature Type: Dark Spirit
Level: 13
Health: 247
Mana: 236

The creature was stronger than before but so was I. Baridorne first drew the shadow's attention with noise and sword, clashing his weapon into his shield just as Clifford had done. When it got close, I signaled to the group to attack.

Cilden, Moga, and Baridorne tossed the healing potions at the creature. The glass shattered and covered it in the healing fluid. It worked. The monster began to screech in response to its health loss. It swung it's arms around in retaliation, striking Baridorne twice and taking off nearly twenty percent of his health. At this point, both Petey and I were planning our next move. While I spent time dual-casting healing seed and preparing to infuse it, he healed Baridorne and launched a second heal at the monster. It also suffered another round of potions-turned-projectiles. I tried to infuse the spell with my mana, focusing on holding some mana back. When I couldn't hold it any longer, I unleashed my restorative splendor and tendrils lashed out at the creature. Its focus turned to me. We were prepared for it. Baridorne and Cilden stood in its way and pushed it into a wall. It didn't attack them. It only wanted to kill me.

Ten seconds and one magnificent bloom later, the creature faded to dust. The cold dissipated from the room and the giant doors swung open for the final time.

"I'm never coming back to this place," I said to the others. "It's too cold here."

They tried to laugh, but their faces had turned pallid and gray. They had never battled a creature of such darkness before.

My head started to spin when I looked into the next chamber. My vision buckled, like looking through a giant magnifying glass. The others began walking into it while I was left standing at the entrance itself overwhelmed by a sense of foreboding.

"You should go in without me," I said to Cilden. He nodded, understanding that it was the room where I had died. "And Cilden, don't say his name."

With the others out of the picture to claim their new prizes, I reviewed the backlog of notifications from the last few fights:

*You have killed a level 6 Cave Rat * 17. +119xp*
*You have killed a level 7 Cave Rat * 14. +126xp*
*You have killed a level 8 Cave Rat * 15. +150xp*

*You have killed a level 9 Cave Rat * 9. +99xp*

*You have killed a level 10 Cave Rat * 5. +65xp*

Congratulations! You have reached level 6! You have 2 attribute points to assign. 307xp to next level.

Congratulations! Your skill with staves has increased to rank 7. .1% additional damage when attacking. .2% additional chance to block.

Congratulations! You have gained rank 10 in Healing Seed II. Your spell has improved to Healing Seed III. Cast this to plant a seed of natural magic in your target to heal them for 3hp per second for 10 seconds. Upon expiration, the target is healed for another 9hp. Mana cost: 25. Cast time: 2.5s Increase the rank of this spell to increase its potency. Can be modified by Wisdom, enchantments, and racial abilities. Can be dispelled.

...

Congratulations! You have gained rank 14 in Healing Seed III.

Congratulations! Your skill with light armor has increased to rank 5. 0.1% increase in damage mitigation and movement speed.

Congratulations! Your skill with stalking has increased to rank 7. .1% increase to stealth.

You have killed a level 13 rock golem. +187xp

Congratulations! You have gained rank 15 in Healing Seed III. This spell has evolved from Novice Healing Seed III to Apprentice Living Seed I. Cast this to plant a seed of natural magic in your target to heal them for 4hp per second for 10 seconds. Upon expiration, the target is healed for another 10hp. Mana cost: 26. Cast time: 2.5s. Increase the rank of this spell to increase its potency. Can be modified by Wisdom, enchantments, and racial abilities. Can be dispelled.

*You have killed a level 7 goblin * 7. +63xp*

*You have killed a level 8 goblin * 5. +55xp*

*You have killed a level 9 goblin * 6. +72xp*

*You have killed a level 10 goblin * 2. +28xp*

Congratulations! You have reached level 7! You have 4 attribute points to assign. 703xp to next level.

Congratulations! You have gained rank 16 in Living Seed I.

Congratulations! Your skill with light armor has increased to rank 6.
0.1% increase in damage mitigation and movement speed.
Congratulations! Your skill with staves has increased to rank 8. .1%
additional damage when attacking. .1% additional chance to block.
You have killed a level 8 goblin * 5. +55xp
You have killed a level 9 goblin * 4. +48xp
You have killed a level 10 goblin. +14xp
You have killed a level 13 jefat. +198xp
Congratulations! You have gained rank 17 in Living Seed I.
Congratulations! You have gained rank 2 in Dual-Casting.
Congratulations! You have gained rank 3 in Mana Infusion.
Congratulations! Your rank in Leadership has increased to rank 7!

I was more than pleased with my progress, taking the opportunity to pull the tome of Nature's Grace from my inventory. I read through the book. Its pages began to turn on their own. The book slammed shut and crumbled to dust, offering me one more notification:

Congratulations! You have learned a new spell: Novice Nature's Grace
I. This spell infuses the wounds of your target with nature magic,
healing 3HP per second for 4 seconds. Mana cost: 10. Cast time: 1
second. This cannot be dispelled. Increase this spell in rank to
increase the potency.

Although overwhelmed with notifications, I was pleased with my advancement. I didn't expect to gain two levels in one dungeon run. I did some quick math in my head. When I received my brand, I had 118 health and received 117 damage. When leaving the barrier, I would receive 234 damage to my health in 30 seconds. I now had 190 health. I needed to heal myself for 44HP in less than 30 seconds to prevent myself from dying. My new Living Seed spell healed for 50HP over 10 seconds. Combining this with even a weak healing potion made passing through the barrier as easy as walking from one room to another. I was confident that I no longer needed to commit my points to Constitution. Instead, I split them: two points to intelligence, one point to wisdom, and one point to luck. My mind became more focused. My connection to my source of magic increase after making my selection.

"Huh," I said aloud after realizing how easy it was to move beyond the barrier, especially with a master's help. Without our plan, though, an escape of hundreds of slaves and a portal out of Elatha would have been impossible. Cilden and the others returned. Petey clutched his find in his hands, struggling to balance all of the items at once. He discovered the same healing spell I had just consumed, a pile of gold, a new uncommon-class staff, and mana and healing potions. I had the others split the potions among themselves. Petey was overjoyed with keeping the staff and spell tome. He shoved it in his inventory, eager to learn it when he hit level 7. I accepted one gold and 30 silver from the group, adding it to my inventory.

Cilden helped me to my feet while the others started towards the path out of the dungeon.

"There's something different about you, isn't there? In general, I mean," he asked me.

I wanted to respond. I wanted my friend to have the same information as Clifford. I couldn't form the words to tell him, though.

"It's alright. I don't need to know why." He was walking beside me, running his fingers over the side of the cave. "In less than a month, you've gained five levels. You resurrected. You possess control over your base skills more than anyone I've ever seen. You understand the mechanics of battle more than any low-level person. Who would have thought to use healing potions against the jefat?"

We walked in silence for another minute while Cilden reviewed my stats and skills page. "And you gain two attribute points per level. You're blessed by the gods, my friend. This much is clear. I don't need to know why. I don't need to know where you've come from. I do know that you have promised to keep my family and me safe. You made it your goal to see my children free again. If I knew nothing else, this would be enough."

He stopped and put his hand on my shoulder, turning me to him. Both Vindur and I were listening to every word he said.

"If it means the safety and survival of my family, I will follow you to the ends of the world. Your goals and mine are aligned. So should our fates be. Like Moga and Baridorne are mine, will you allow me to be your ally and companion?"

"I would never think of saying no. From the moment you clothed me, you showed me your heart. You and your family were at your lowest point in your lives. You were forced into slavery because you were in the wrong place at the wrong time. We're not only friends. We're family. If something were to happen to you and Rose, your children would want for nothing. They will always have a family to take care of them as long as I am in their lives."

Congratulations! Your dedication to Cilden Thatcher and his family means you have a family of your own. Your disposition towards him has increased from Trusted to Companion. Your interest and fates are now combined. Do not forsake your companions. Doing so comes at a great cost to you both. +150xp received.

Now that Cilden was my ally and companion, Vindur was able to reveal himself. The man fell backward, his back sliding against the cold wall of the cage.

"Don't worry, Cilden." I shared my story with my friend; my story of Earth. I explained its technology, my family, my friends, my work, my death, and my rebirth. I revealed my blessing and my curse.

"If what you're saying is true, I'm glad to have you around. If you didn't show up, Neeta would most likely be a slave the rest of her life. We're going to get out of this, you and I. We'll find a way to be free."

Cilden spent the rest of the time telling me stories of his young adulthood. He was born in the same village he was captured in. He had gone out hunting with Moga when they stumbled on an elven camp. It was there he met Rose. The moment he saw her, the two were inseparable. Despite the Elders of her village protesting, Rose decided to marry Cilden. She was exiled from her clan as a result. A few years later, Junta was born. Neeta followed a year after that. They thought they had built a quiet and safe life for themselves. They were mistaken.

I made a promise that night to return to them their stolen life. Cilden wasn't a warrior at heart. He was a farmer. Rose was a mother and healer. I swore to him that I would help him find his vocation again.

> *You have received a quest! "The land is my home." You have promised to make Cilden a farmer again. You will have six months to accomplish this quest. This quest is not optional.*
> *Reward: Unknown.*

Secret name: Slanaitheoir (savior)
Character name: Michael Dian-Cecht
Race: Spirit Elf
Age: 27
Class: Undefined
Talent: Undefined
Level 7 (377xp to next level)
Health: 190 (170)
Mana: 213 (168)
Stamina: 170
Fatigue: 15%
Armor: 37 (.5% damage mitigation) - 1.5% damage mitigation with skills.
Strength: 12
Intelligence: 15
Wisdom: 14
Constitution: 16
Agility: 12
Luck: 6
Alignment: Chaotic Good (+1)
Racial Traits: +5% to herbalism, +5% to all non-metal crafting, +5% to nature-based healing and damage spells, +5% to mana regeneration
Profession: Undefined
Company: Undefined
Modifiers: +10% movement speed, Spirit Elf (+10% to all damage and healing done. -10% to all magical damage taken. +10% increase to all physical damage taken)

Skills:
Novice Blades 1
Novice Staves 8
Novice Grappling 1 (1% increase damage)
Novice Light Armor 6(1% reduced damage/movement speed)
Novice Observation 6

Novice Stalking 7 (1.6% chance of remaining hidden)
Novice Herbalism 3
Novice Tailoring 1
Novice Tracking 1
Notice Leadership

Spells:
Novice Nature's Grace I.
Apprentice Living Seed I
Novice Dual-Cast (rank 2)
Novice Mana infusion (rank 3)
Spirit Trek (no rank)

13

_____

As promised, I never returned to Nott's Sanctum. I couldn't bring myself to go back there. Cilden visited it dozens of times and had gained another level. I swore to Rose that I would help her create potions. And we did. We spent our days producing dozens of concoctions for weeks on end. I continued to gain more and more experience. Potion creation was second-nature to me. When I played the game, I had made it my profession. It had saved me countless times in battle. At one point, I thought about pursuing enchanting, but why focus on making what I could easily buy? Potions were different. A practical application of herbs created limitless potential. You could create almost anything if you had the aptitude and knowledge. A Grandmaster Herbalist could send his enemies fleeing from the battlefield. He could also save people from death's grip with healing concoctions that could resurrect them when administered in time.

I woke up in the morning, cleaned up, made breakfast, and joined Rose in the kitchen for a day filled with crushing herbs and brewing mixtures. Neeta and Junta ran in and out all day bringing us plants they had found. By this time, they were able to harvest herbs from many gardens, the masters of those homes friendly to our cause. When Rose reached rank 15 and became an apprentice in Herbalism, I was already at rank 22. We began by making higher-quality healing potions using ginseng root, lavender, and sage.

Lavender was easy to use if you knew the trick. Long ago, I learned that it had to be dried. Only then, could the leaves be massaged in your hands, broken into small pieces. The flakes of the flower and stem contained the mana ready to be released—a potent concoction willing to tell some other ingredient what to do. That is where the sage came in. Unlike jasmine, sage leaves wouldn't release their mana easily. One had to make an oil with the sage. The leaves first had to be washed and dried. Then you mixed the leaves with hot olive oil. The mixture had to sit for two weeks before it was ready to be used in potions.

"But what about the olives?" Rose asked. She remembered my lesson about the wooden spoon.

"If you crush or mince olives and add it to a mixture, it releases its mana into your creation. If you press the olives and collect their oil, the mana is already released into the earth. Because of this, oil—any oil—is a repository. You can coax it into accepting the characteristics and mana of another ingredient."

"And the lavender? What makes it a better healing herb than jasmine?"

"Healing power is absorbed into the plant by its flower. Lavender has more buds. Because it's closer to the stem, you have to treat it with more care. Jasmine is simple. You massage the petals with a mortar, and it releases its mana. Lavender is stubborn. It needs to be weakened and dried. Only then will it give you its mana. If it is moist and alive, it will protect its mana by sending it into the plant. When that happens, the potion will be useless."

"And sage? Where does that come in?"

"Sage is funny. When made into a tea, it can do any number of things. It prevents memory loss in elders. It can also prevent flatulence."

"I'll have to remember that one for my husband," Rose joked.

"I'm sure he'll be glad for that. As I was saying, the sage plant stores its mana in the leaves. In a pinch, you can crush the leaves in some water, and it will help staunch bleeding. It can also clean sores. Sage is a much more potent medicinal herb. It replaces jasmine. It is also out of control. When mixed with just ginseng, the potion is more likely to cure a poison than it is to heal wounds. It needs to be made into oil. Only then can it receive instruction from the lavender. The lavender tells it to focus just on wounds. That's why this recipe is more complex. We couldn't make it at rank 1. Now that you're rank 15, it'll be easier."

And so we began to prepare. We had enough dry jasmine to last us a lifetime thanks to Clifford. We crushed the jasmine in our mortar, mixing in a few drops of sage oil that I had prepared in the previous weeks. After the ingredients had merged into one, we added it to the ginseng root tea and let it simmer for a few hours. Once ready, we strained the ingredients into a small vial to produce our first, new healing potion.

You have created (2) Lesser Healing Potions. Quality: Good. Class: Uncommon. When consumed, restores 30 health over 15 seconds. +8xp.

"Why did we make two this time?

"They mix better with the water. You can try to make another one, but I doubt the mixture will be potent enough to form a potion. The mana drains out quickly."

The two of us had a long way to go before we could successfully make our first invisibility potion. Even my knowledge wasn't enough. This world operated on crunching numbers and creative calculations. At rank 30 we could make the mixture. We still only had a 25% chance of success then.

By the end of the day, we created four more batches of lesser healing potions. Rose and I both increased another level. I split my two attribute points between Intelligence and Wisdom. We were doing a happy dance when the others joined us. Cilden, Petey, Moga, and Baridorne were caked in grime and dirt. We were clean and fresh, dancing in the kitchen like children celebrating Christmas morning.

I had a surprise for my friends tonight. I kicked everyone but Rose out of the kitchen.

"Tonight, my dear lady, we're going to create something new; something from my homeland."

She looked at me with shock in her eyes. In the last two months, I never showed any interest in cooking or preparing dinner. I had a hankering for something more delectable. Roasted meat and vegetables were excellent and all, but they only fed my stomach. I needed some comfort food, something with a doughy crust, tomatoes, and cheese.

While Rose rolled out the dough, I cut any free cheese into pieces small enough to melt. I chopped up some onions, olives, spinach, and smoked ham and set them aside. Finally, I added crushed tomatoes and chopped garlic into a pot. Tomato sauce was born. The entire time, Rose was looking at me like I was insane. I was whistling "Always Look On The Bright Side of Life" while prepping the food, excited to witness my creation being born.

I added as much wood to the oven as I dared. There was so much heat emanating from it that Rose thought the house would burn down.

"It's fine," I said as I poured my sauce, cheese, and ingredients over the thinly pressed dough.

"What is it?"

"It's called a pizza!"

We made ten of them in total, putting each one in the oven until the ingredients cooked and the bread turned into a crispy, brown crust.

You have created Pizza * 10. Item quality: Good. Item class: Epic.
Consuming one serving of pizza reduces fatigue by 15%. +30xp
Congratulations! You have learned a new skill. Cooking (rank 5). You
can create delectable dishes that are better able to reduce fatigue.
Increase in rank to improve the quality of your creations.

Cilden, Moga, Baridorne, Clifford, and the children were all waiting at the door. They were drawn there like sailors attracted to a siren. The scent of roasted tomatoes, cheese, and garlic had penetrated every corner of the estate. We had to push the others away from us to get the food upstairs where the remainder of the slaves were waiting for dinner. Twenty-five slaves, our soon-to-be ex-master and a handful of guards filled the table, stuffing their faces with my new creation. They hardly took the time to breathe, many of them raising their glasses shouting "Three cheers to the chef!" With everyone satisfied, Clifford and I abandoned the group to retire to his bedroom. I hadn't spoken to him at length since my last and final visit to Nott's Sanctum.

With the door latched behind us, I grabbed him by the waist, lifted myself up on the balls of my feet, and kissed him. He returned the gesture with both compassion and eagerness. The fireplace was roaring when we entered the room. I began to sweat from the heat. We both removed our shirts and laid down on the bed, looking up at the sky. He had an exposed skylight half as wide as the bed. The view was disconcerting. Purple lines radiated across the sky, weaving in and out of the entrapment dome surrounding Elatha. The purple energy lit up the sky every night. Mages in the palace poured their dark magic into the spell, making sure that no slave in the city could escape while no citizen could find hope in the light of day.

"It's something, isn't it?" I asked Clifford, turning to look at him. I needed an excuse to not look at the barrier.

"It is. My father wanted me trained to be a Maintainer. They're honored and respected members of the court. He was furious with me when I refused." Clifford returned his attention to me, tracing my muscles with his fingers from my neck to my belly button. His rough skin rubbing against my smooth torso tantalized me, sending chills through my body.

"Is that any different than his usual disposition?" I asked with a coy smile on my face.

"Cheeky!" He gently pinched my nipple to punish me for my wit. "This isn't entirely his fault. My father holds the rule of law in high regard. He's also greedy by nature. I'm sure that if slavery were abolished, he wouldn't care one bit. He only owns a handful of slaves himself."

He was massaging my entire torso now, his fingers slowly tracing a line between each of my ribs.

"Enough about my father. And about the barrier. I don't want to talk about it tonight."

I nodded, abandoning conversation for the moment at hand. Clifford and I spent the rest of the night in his bedroom. We enjoyed one another like we enjoyed the pizza: completely and with abandon. It was only when the fire died that we resigned ourselves to sleep, giving respite to our aching and fatigued bodies.

The next two months were about the same. The children gathered herbs to complete their daily quest. Cilden and the others took novice healers into Nott's sanctum to level them up, given them other healing spells, and collect HP rings. They had to stop for a time. Guards became suspicious after seeing the same three slaves in the outer ring multiple times, despite being escorted by a master. The three of them and the children had also gained a level.

Rose and I spent our days in the kitchen brewing potions. I had increased to Journeyman rank 37. She had reached rank 30, spending many sleepless nights preparing ingredients and crafting solutions in a futile effort to catch up to me. By the time we were ready to review invisibility elixirs, we had already filled our quota of healing potions, over 300 of them lining a shelf on the far side of the room.

I sat in my rickety chair, elbows on the kitchen table. In front of me were the ingredients I needed for the invisibility potion: moon grass, jasmine flower, wisp root, and fresh water collected under a full moon. I scratched the skin under my slave collar. Although the replica wasn't as rough as my original, it did irritate my skin. I wanted to remove it, but Clifford warned us all to keep them on at all times, even when sleeping and bathing. He let me remove it when we bathed together. I was glad for that.

"Now you're going to have to explain these ingredients again. I didn't get it the first time."

"You mean the first three times," I snapped back. Rose slapped me in the back of the head, warning me not to be smart.

"Alright. Let's start with the ingredient translation. Most potions and elixirs need a delivery component. Roots are the easiest. Moss can also work in some cases. For invisibility potions, it's important to have an ingredient that can deliver the magical properties of the drink quickly. Ginseng root can't do this. The result would be only partial invisibility."

I grabbed the wisp root in my hand and began separating the strands of the roots carefully. "Now these roots are also fragile. That's why invisibility is broken whenever you take any damage. Because of their fragile nature, you have to be careful when loosening the root ball. If you break any roots off, the magic will leave the sample. If you use the roots when they're all balled up, the potion won't work."

"Like combing hair?"

"Yes. Like combing hair." She whacked me again, accusing me of being fresh.

Ignoring her protest, I continued with my explanation. "Now the jasmine serves a different purpose compared to a healing potion. With the healing potion, we only cared about the mana in the petals. This time, we need the mana in the stamen and pistil." Rose had a blank expression on her face. "That's the male and female parts of the flower."

"Flowers don't have a gender."

"Yes. They do. They have both. At the same time. You're just going to have to trust me on this."

Even though she didn't believe me, she respected my knowledge.

"We care about these parts of the flower precisely because they contain the most potent mana. It is too strong for healing potions and would overwhelm the recipe. For invisibility potions, though, it's a perfect fit. This is also an incredibly fragile ingredient. To release the mana, we need to steam it for less than five seconds. Once the mana is released, you have less than a moment to mix it with the other ingredients."

"And the moon grass?"

"The moon grass is less sensitive. Just beat it into a pulp, and it will be ready. Because it has absorbed mana from the moon, it is the best ingredient we have to tell the wisp roots what to do. It'll convey properties that will bend light around anyone who consumes the potion. Only, it doesn't have enough mana to say it loudly enough."

"Hence the moon water."

I was struck dumb by Rose's unprompted insight. I could only offer her a blank expression. I caught her hand when she tried to hit me.

"You got it! You finally got it!" I yelled, standing up to spin her around in a happy dance.

I let go of her hand after she relaxed. She had a giant grin on her face, pleased that she understood an ingredient before I explained it to her.

The two of us began to prepare the concoction. We beat the moon grass into a fine paste, carefully massaging the paste into the untangled wisp roots. I had to setup a different cooking system for this. We had one big pot over the fire, the water at a rolling boil. On the surface of the water were two small pots containing steaming moon water. Adding the moon grass and wisp root to the smaller pots, we carefully peeled off the bits of the jasmine we needed and held it over the steam until the small stalks began to sweat. Rose followed my instruction and dumped the jasmine into the mixture.

I placed my metal spoon in the pot and began rotating the water, trying my best not to break any of the roots. After a minute, foam formed on the top of the water. I carefully spooned the foam into a glass vial I held in my other hand careful not to spill any of the precious fluid in the process.

The bubbles in the foam began to dissolve, allowing a green liquid to settle at the bottom of the vial. With the foam gone, the flask was about one-eighth full.

"That's it? Not even an entire potion?"

I looked at Rose while I put a stopper in the vial. "Yup. We have to do this eight or nine times—At least until we receive a notification. If the vial fills before receiving one, the creation has failed."

And fail it did. Over and over again. It took us forty batches before our first success.

You have created (1) Lesser Invisibility Potion. Quality: Good. Class: Rare. Must mix with one drop of blood from the imbiber. When consumed, provides 30 minutes of invisibility. Any damage or healing received breaks invisibility.

We brewed for a few more hours. I prepared the ingredients while Rose made the potion. She was about to quit for the night, too tired and flustered to do anything else. I convinced her to finish one more vial. On her last batch, she received the notification informing her of her success. The little elf started dancing around the kitchen, shaking her hips to celebrate her victory. I was pleased with my student, not only because she mastered a new potion. She also learned from me the fantastic art of the "happy dance."

When she calmed down, she sat in a chair across from me, clutching the vial in her hands.

"You know, a part of me thought our plan was doomed to fail. Holding this potion in my hand now, I feel we can do it." Her attitude grew sullen. "When the soldiers came that night, I thought our lives were over. I imagined a life where our children and grandchildren were resigned to servitude." She examined the vessel, the cloudy liquid coating the sides of the glass.

"And now we have a chance to be free again. Thanks to you. What you have accomplished here is unbelievable. I first saw you when you were level 2. I saw too much of you for my liking. I thought you were wretched." She set the vial down on the table and grabbed my hand, leaning forward to look into my eyes.

"But you went out of your way to help us when we were at our lowest point. You've made us stronger and better than we were before. My daughter trusts you. My husband has sworn to follow you the rest of his days. He even told me you promised to make him a farmer again! Is there no end to your compassion and kindness?"

She hushed me before I could answer.

"I know I was slow to like you. It's always been particularly challenging for me to make friends with other elves after the way my village treated me. I found love. And because of who I found it with, I was exiled. But you're different than other elves."

She sighed. She was trying to get the right words out but was rambling.

"What I'm trying to say is that I trust you, my young friend. I believe in you. Only time will reveal whether my faith is justified. If we all get out of here alive, you may count me among your allies."

Congratulations! Your disposition with Rose Thatcher has increased from Friendly to Trusted.

"I have no doubt that we're all going to get out of here." Rose and I both turned towards the source of the voice at the entrance to the kitchen. It was Nila Hislop. "But we have a problem."

Clifford was standing in the doorway behind her. He stared at me with a tinge of stress in his eyes, tension lines casting shadows across his forehead. The two of them had just returned from the palace where, until recently, they had spent most of their days. They were wearing the forest green cassocks unique to learned scholars, trimmed with gold thread and a golden sash. We followed them upstairs to Clifford's study at their request. Cilden and the others were waiting for us there, whispering quietly among themselves.

Normally, the room had a comfortable lounge area where I had spent a few evenings reading one of the thousands of books Clifford had collected over the course of his life. Instead of sofas and end tables, the area was stripped bare save a round table. Two maps were pinned to the surface of the table. A map of Elatha was on the left with various markers and notes penned onto it, dictating the location and head-count of slaves planning an escape. It also had individual paths to be taken to get the slaves out of the inner ring of the city with minimal notice.

The second map was a regional one. I recognized the text above a red marker. It was the area around the ruins Clifford planned for our new home.

My lover and master stood by my side. I felt his body press up against mine as we both looked on the maps Nila had procured. She stood opposite us chewing on her lip, trying to come up with the right words to say.

The tension in the room was so thick you could drown in it. I was about to speak up and ask a question when Nila finally broke the silence.

"Our little plan hasn't gone unnoticed," she said, her eyes fixed on the map of Elatha below. "Apparently, some guards have picked up on an average level increase among the slave population. We're only lucky they haven't decided to go door to door to take a census. If they did, we wouldn't be here now."

She sat down in a nearby chair, having lost all the color in her face. She nodded to Clifford to continue.

"We've just come from a council meeting at the palace. While the guards want to perform this census, enough of us were able to lodge a complaint, suggesting that the invasion of our privacy was a high cost to pay for an unverified suspicion."

He left my side and walked over to the entrance of his balcony, looking out at the city below.

"They did, however, decide on one course of action. The Protectorate is going to ask the Maintainers to increase the strength of the spell. When complete, the spell will deal triple the amount of damage instead of double."

A wave of silence overwhelmed the room again. Cilden was holding Rose in her arms, the elf woman overwhelmed at the thought of exposing her children to such a risk.

I coughed a bit in shock. I knew what this meant. Even if we pooled all of our resources together, it would be almost impossible to get the core group of us through the barrier alive. No one wanted to break the silence. It was my plan. I had to.

"What does this mean?" Nila and Clifford both ignored me, unsure of how to answer my question.

"What I mean is... how is this done? How do they make the barrier more efficient? And why haven't they done it already if it's so easy?"

"It's not easy," Nila said. "It requires all maintainers at once. Even then, they need to draw from an immense source of mana to accomplish it. It's not like flipping a switch. The spell to amplify the barrier takes hours to complete."

I mulled over her response with great care.

"This is perfect," I said. I heard a few whispers from the others in the room. Clifford knew the way my mind worked, however. The corners of his mouth upturned. He motioned for me to continue.

"My guess is that they're going to need all of the masters present to do this. They have to get the mana from somewhere, right? No group of slaves is going to offer enough to fuel the spell when compared to the collective mana of the masters. Right?"

Nila nodded.

"Which means that for a few hours on the night of the casting, slaves will be left unattended. And the guards will be too distracted at the palace to notice the movement of a few hundred, invisible slaves!"

"What you're suggesting is risky. We'll be moving hundreds of people through a barrier that could amplify at any point. Half of you could be trapped inside before escaping."

I dismissed her complaints with a wave of my hand. Her brow furrowed at the gesture, the master in her taking over for a brief moment.

"We'll just have to start earlier. And without as many invisibility potions. When are they planning on doing this?"

"One week," Clifford said. He had now returned to my side as I began moving markers around on the map.

"So here is what we'll do." The entire group was standing over the table listening to my new plan. When I reviewed it, I noticed that Clifford and Cilden listened earnestly and thoroughly, trusting every word I was saying. The others were more skeptical. I was able to convince them in the end.

Congratulations! Your rank in Leadership has increased to 10. You are now able to form raid groups consisting of 25 members. Improve this skill further to gain additional perks and rewards.

14

"I have a surprise for you," Clifford said to me from one room over. I woke up on the morning of our great escape in a zombie-like daze, unable to sleep well the night before. My heart was racing all night as I pictured every possible avenue for failure in my head. I stepped through the plan detail by detail, shaking Clifford awake every time I hit a significant doubt or roadblock.

Vindur had long since abandoned me, choosing to sleep on the ground in front of the fireplace instead.

At 5 AM, Clifford ordered me out of bed. I took the opportunity to draw a bath, hoping that the warm water and steam would calm me down. I must have fallen asleep in the tub. His voice startled me awake, causing me to thrash around in the water wondering where I was.

Lifting myself out of the tub was agonizing. Crisp air assaulted my body. My nipples became erect in response to the cold. I looked around for a towel, but there was none. The escape plan required all of our attention in the last week. Menial tasks like laundry and cleaning and cooking served no purpose now.

Walking back into the bedroom, I was dripping on the floor. I looked like a wet dog. My silver hair matted against my head, cold streams of water running down my chest and back. I shivered like a child getting out of a pool.

"Unless you're going to tell me that they screwed up and the barrier vanished, I've no interest in your surprises. Your last big surprise killed me, remember?"

He tossed me a damp towel that he had used the night before. It was mostly ineffective but managed to soak up some of the remaining water on my body. Casting the towel over my shoulder, I stumbled over to the other side of the room to see what Clifford was arranging on the table. When I got closer, he draped his arm around me. His hand settled on my exposed backside. The warmth of his torso was enough to scare away my shivers.

On the table in front of me, Clifford had neatly laid out a new set of clothing and armor. I couldn't say anything. I was stricken with silence, my mouth hanging open in shock.

"Things are going to be dangerous tonight. I don't want you to have to worry about the barrier or your ability to heal."

"It's too much," I mumbled to him, feeling more like a house boy with him as my sugar daddy.

"No, it's not. You're risking everything for your friends. That's too much. This just cost me money that I don't need." He pulled me closer to him. I could tell he was nervous about the risk we were all going to take tonight. "Now. Put it on. Unless you're going to do this naked, which is more likely to end up in your getting arrested before you even reach the barrier."

Staff of Druid's Healing. Quality: Exquisite. Class: Epic. Damage: 25-31 DPS. Can be broken by stronger weapons. Stats: +60 MP, +3% increase to healing and damage spells.

Tailored Scholar's Hooded-Shirt. Quality: Professional. Class: Uncommon. Armor: Light(5). +5MP. +20% to stealth when wearing the hood. Can be destroyed by weapons.

Nurturer's Leather Jerkin. Quality: Exquisite. Class: Rare. Armor: Light(20). Stats: +20 MP, +20 HP, +2% increase to healing and damage spells. Set: 1 of 4

Nurturer's Leather Pants. Quality: Professional. Class: Rare. Armor:

Light(15). Stats: +20 MP, +20HP, +2% increase to healing and
damage spells. Set: 2 of 4

Nurturer's Leather boots. Quality: Exquisite. Class: Rare. Armor:
Light(10). Stats: +20% movement speed, +10HP. Set: 3 of 4

Nurturer's Leather Bracers. Quality: Exquisite. Class: Rare. Armor:
Light(10). Stats: +15 HP Set: 4 of 4

Mana-Dowsed Ring of Protection. Quality: Exquisite. Class: Epic.
+35MP. Trigger to cast a protective barrier over a target that
mitigates 25% of incoming damage for 30 seconds. Charges: 5/5.
This item gains one charge per day until full.

Ring of Spell Storage. Quality: Exquisite. Class: Epic. Stores one spell
for later use. This ring can only be filled once per day.

I placed my old armor and staff into my inventory. It was now half full. I could feel the weight of the added items pull on my shoulder, although even at maximum capacity my inventory would not be substantial enough to slow me down.

Clifford helped me put on my clothes and items. The green leather pants were the first. Although usually opposed to leather pants, these felt more like cotton. They hugged my body, stretching with me. The pants were not constricting and extended with ease when I moved.

The scholar's shirt was next. It was a simple, black v-neck shirt that cut off at the shoulders. I wasn't used to wearing something that left my arms exposed, but I saw the advantage it offered for spell casting and wielding a staff. The shirt also had a hood that could be worn to activate additional effects.

The brown leather jerkin wore like a glove, bending with my torso without catching or pulling. It was stitched together with a shining silver-green thread. The vest had green straps and jade buttons.

The green leather bracers were also soft and comfortable. I wasn't sure how Clifford managed it. The bracers seemed to settle on my skin. They didn't shift or slide when I swung my arms.

The boots were most welcome of them all. My old boots felt stiff and were hard to walk in, like newly bought hiking boots. These made me feel like I was walking around barefoot, but offered all the protection of a heavier shoe.

When I fastened the final lace in the boots, I received a notification.

You have equipped a full set of armor: Nurturer's Regalia. +20 armor
bonus. +20HP, +20MP, +10% mana regeneration, 25% threat
reduction.

Standing in front of the mirror, I recalled the last four months of my life. I had come so far since I woke up naked in the woods. I ran my fingers over the slave mark on my shoulder. In less than twelve hours, the magic contained within it would activate. Only the spent scar would remain.

Clifford stood behind me, both of his hands on my shoulders. We stood in front of a mirror, thinking about how far we had come. In less than four months, this man developed an uncanny ability to understand what I was feeling. He made sure that I was not feeling alone.

"Are you ready?" he asked, pressing himself against my back.

"No. I'm not. But that's not going to stop me."

We left his bedroom for the final time, its fireplace cold. The room was both unnerving and dark. It was as far from the sanctuary it had become for me. Some books were missing, filed away in Clifford's inventory. Aside from his clothing, he hadn't packed much else.

The home was missing its usual flurry of activity. Darkness and silence enveloped the entire estate. The last seven days saw Clifford's house transformed into a stop on an underground railroad of sorts. Every morning, a master arrived with a group of slaves from his or her household. Cilden, Moga, or Baridorne escorted them to Nott's Sanctum and helped them purge the dungeon of all threats. They used our stronger healing potions to bring down the jefat. Once there, the group remained with enough food and water to last the remainder of the week.

Each visit to the dungeon spawned a new instance. By the end of the week, almost 250 slaves were waiting patiently, ready to exit when the time was right.

Rose and I had been able to create hundreds of invisibility potions and healing potions, distributing them among the remaining slaves who were going to sneak their way to the barrier in less than ten hours.

I didn't gain a new level, but my Herbalism skill increased to rank 45. We had planned for household guards to escort them in groups of ten. A city guard would be less suspicious if he saw a private guard walking down the street. Convincing them wasn't difficult. Their pockets were lined with more gold than they earned in a decade.

We also distributed food, seeds, weapons, and tools to each adult slave. One slave even agreed to fill his entire inventory with a single anvil. They carried everything we needed to establish a new home and sanctuary in the woods, well outside of the watchful gaze of the masters in Elatha.

When today rolled around, there was nothing left to do besides waiting. So I did. We all waited in the courtyard with the gates closed. I took the time to observe each of my friends.

Junta was sitting with his father in silence. He was old enough to understand what we were doing. His face was sullen, apprehensive at the idea of experiencing the same pain he felt when he received the brand. He scratched at the scar on his shoulder. Earlier in the day, I had given him my old bracers and chest piece. Although he was only six, the human half of him made him nearly the same size as me. He was built much like his father, with a long and wide torso. Cilden helped him fit the armor, pleased that his son would have more than enough health to see him through the barrier with only a single healing potion.

Neeta was sitting between Rose and me. The little girl was playing with shiny rings on her fingers. We had to tie them all together with string, anchoring the rings to her wrist like a glove. They would have otherwise slipped off. The idea of her daughter losing the rings made Rose nervous, but I played a little game with Neeta where I had her hold onto a "magic stone." I told her that if she clutched it in her hand and remained completely silent, the stone would turn into a gold coin in five hours. She loved the idea of the game. It would keep the rings from sliding off and keep her silent at the same time.

Moga was perched in his usual spot, shoulder pressed into the cold alabaster pillars by the front door. He had nothing to say. Hell. He had nothing to do, waiting eagerly to be gone from this place.

Baridorne was playing a card game with some older children in the group. I wanted to move all of the children ahead of time. Nila overruled me, though. The guards were already suspicious. Moving all of the children would risk exposing our plan. She was right. I found myself trusting her guidance more every day.

Petey sat on the edge of the fountain beside me. I had come to know the young Trisian quite well in the prior months. He was born a slave. In his short years, he worked in the mines. He was once sold to a whorehouse to pay off his owner's debt. Nila saw him one day and felt pity for the boy. She bought him for twice his value only to save him. I spent a few days with Petey over the last few months teaching him new healing techniques. He was thrilled to learn them, excited to be seen as something more than a slave. He even earned validation and respect from our household, running potions and messages from one ally to another.

Clifford and Nila were standing at the front gate reviewing the final details of the plan. The two were hashing through last minute details. Clifford cracked the front gate open, surveying the square in front of his soon to be abandoned home.

"I could have resurrected anywhere," I said to Vindur. "And if I had, these people would be slaves the rest of their lives."

Vindur and I hadn't talked much in the last few weeks. He spent more and more time off my shoulder. I was grateful for having him in my life, but he was my guide. What would he do absent guiding me? The moment the thought entered my head, the lemur shot up.

"I wondered how long it would take you," he said to me with a smile on his face.

"You mean you could hear my thoughts this whole time?"

"Yes. I learned enough to know you haven't needed me for a while now. I only stuck around until you realized it." He jumped from his resting place between my legs and wrapped his arms around my neck, nuzzling his cheek to mine.

"I have every confidence, my young friend, that you will transform this world. You will make it better again, first in Vros and then beyond. That is why Balama put you here. She also named you Slanaitheoir. This is an ancient name. The goddess poured through thousands of tomes while your spirit was asleep. She looked at your life on earth. She looked at your actions in Fjorgyn. She gave you this name to signal the rebirth of goodness into the world. Her choice took almost a century to make. All the while, your spirit rested in a gentle sleep."

His words struck me more than they should have. It didn't matter what amount of time passed between my death and rebirth. It drove the final nail into my earthly coffin. Even if I were to somehow return to earth, there would be nothing and no one to return to. Tears started to fill my eyes. Some escaped, sliding down my cheek to end up trapped in the corners of my mouth.

"Don't be sad, my dear man. Those you left behind on Earth lived lives full of both sadness and joy. You had nieces and nephews who knew your name. Their descendents still think about their uncle, wishing they had known you."

Clifford had walked over. He and Rose saw me starting to cry and tried to comfort me. I willed Vindur to appear to them. Rose withdrew at first, frightened by the sudden appearance of the creature.

A bell started ringing in the distance, signaling the invitation to the palace.

"And so it begins," Vindur said. "This is going to be your brightest hour yet. I would see you to the very end, but you know you don't need me." He began to fade away. I reached out to him.

"I don't want you to go," I said, choking back the tears.

"And that is why I must," the little lemur responded, his hand wrapped around my index finger. "My purpose was to serve you while you needed me. You no longer do. You have other guides to help you." He nodded towards Clifford and Rose.

"Goodbye, my friend."

"Farewell, fried chicken."

Vindur let out one final laugh. A silver light encompassed his body and turned it to dust. What remained of him was carried away by a wisp of wind.

The moment clouded my mind. My first real friend in Fjorgyn was now gone. I was on my own. And I wasn't. I wiped the tears from my face and looked at both Rose and Clifford. "Let's do this."

～

There was a flurry of activity outside Clifford's estate after the bells started chiming. Masters were being called to the palace, this time without their slaves. Some were walking on foot. Others had horses. Some were carried in litters, guards straining to carry the weight of their obese lords. Each master had a look of smug satisfaction on their face. I wanted to punch each and every one of them. I only hesitated because I knew doing so would break the invisibility effect.

There was a problem with my plan that became immediate. Aside from the occasional footprint in the mud, I couldn't tell where anyone was. I could only feel Neeta pressed into my chest, her hand clutching the same "magical stone" I had given her earlier.

This stone better work, I thought to myself. It was going to cost me a gold piece.

Even Clifford and Nila took the potions. They couldn't be seen moving away from the palace against the flow of traffic. It would raise suspicions. They would be turned back by the guards.

We reached the first wall. A giant red gate was left open on its hinges. The wall was fifty feet high. Four main gates leading into the inner ring were our only known escape. Even then, we were limited to only two. The others were too far from Nott's Sanctum.

Our escorts stopped when they reached the gate to be questioned by the city guards. I held air in my lungs, afraid that my breathing would reveal me. One of our escorts made an excuse about leaving the inner ring, suggesting that slaves from his household were still at the market.

"Either they get a lashing when we get back, or I do. I don't have time for this. My Lord demands his slaves be back before he returns." The man pulled at his chest plate, engraved with the owl sigil of the Grey household. He pressed a few coins into the city guard's hand as a bribe.

While this entire exchange was going on, the guard was distracted. We took this opportunity to sneak through the gate. Or I did, at least. I couldn't see anyone else. I had stopped to wait for our escort when an invisible force bumped into me.

"Michael?"

"Cilden?"

"You have Neeta?"

"Yeah."

"Good. Let's go."

Before a full hour had passed, I gave Neeta one of her invisibility potions, taking the time to drink one of mine. In the corner of my vision, I saw the countdown renew. We earned sixty more minutes of invisibility. The palace bells had stopped ringing. The ritual itself would begin soon. We had three hours to complete our escape and were still an hour from Nott's Sanctum.

As we continued to walk, I bumped into other invisible forces. First I found Rose and Junta. Rose was clutching her son's hand afraid to lose him. Ten minutes later, I bumped into Nila. I only knew from the smell of her: a lavender perfume that reminded me of the gardens in the inner ring. I tried to ask her where Clifford was. She hushed me. Her footprints trailed away.

Upon reaching the outer ring, the stone buildings gave way to wood. I couldn't see any guards. As I thought, they were all pulled into the inner rings to keep an eye on the slaves while the masters were away. By now, the markets had closed. Stalls were empty, and corridors were deserted. I saw dozens of footprints in the mud, some fresh. I could hear whispers and chatters around me—other groups of slaves making their way to the dungeon.

Neeta and I took our third and final invisibility potion. Our goal was within reach. We approached a fork in the road and saw a city guard talking to one of our escorts. Behind him, I assumed slaves waited, ready to pounce on the guard should he become suspicious.

"I told you. I'm waiting for the young master of my house. They're down at the Sanctum. Should be back any minute now."

"Nonsense! You said he went there this morning. Either your lord is dead, or he doesn't exist. Since there hasn't been a reported death at Nott's in years, I demand you tell me the truth!"

I thought the slaves were about to escape when I saw Clifford appear down the road, running up to the two guards.

"Ahh, my escort. There you are! I thought I told you to wait by the entrance to the dungeon. What are you doing up here?"

The escort was at a loss for words. The deception was shallow. The guard wasn't from his house.

"Aren't you supposed to be in the inner ring? If any of my father's slaves attempt an escape tonight, you'll be sorry! What's your name? Who is your commanding officer?"

The city guard stood erect when confronted by an aristocrat.

"As I thought. Go on, then! Get back to your post before someone misses you."

The guard almost dropped his spear when he spun around and took off. Once he was a safe distance away, I walked up to Clifford and poked him in the side. Watching him jump was enough to make Neeta laugh. His yelp echoed down the side of the valley leading toward the dungeon.

I reached out and took his hand, pulling him behind me.

It took us thirty minutes to reach the bottom of the hill. By that time, the area was crowded with slaves, each one hugging the face of the cliff. They stayed as far away from the barrier as possible.

Once we were sure that no guards would spot us, I pressed my hand into a sharp rock on the side of the cliff, breaking my skin and taking minor damage. I looked awkward, clutching a still invisible Neeta in my arms. Once I became visible, others followed suit: Rose first, then Junta, then Nila, Cilden, Petey, Moga, and Baridorne.

I did a rough head count to be sure. All twenty-five slaves from our household were present. I couldn't count everyone, but there were at least one-hundred more waiting, the barrier repelling them to the cliff.

More started pouring out of Nott's Sanctum by the minute.

My friends were looking at me, baiting me to take charge.

"Alright," I said, loud enough for everyone around me to hear me. "Let's begin by saying the obvious. We have to pass through this barrier. And we need to do it quickly. It's going to hurt. I'm not going to lie about that."

Some people clutched their shoulders when I said this. Many still remembered the pain they experienced when receiving the brand.

"It's important that none of you try to cross the barrier without verbal approval from a healer. The moment before you cross it, drink a healing potion. We will be watching you. If you need one, we will cast a healing spell on you. If you need another one, that will also happen. No one is going to die tonight. We're going to make it."

The crowd's energy improved. I even saw some of them smile. I spotted another thirty to forty heads appearing out of thin air.

"It looks like we're all almost here. And no alarms are sounding. This is good news.

"This is the most important thing I have to tell you. Whatever you do, do not cry out in pain. I know it'll be difficult. Bite into your shirt if you must. Scream into your arm if it helps. Crying out will make noise. And noise will attract the guards."

I handed the still-invisible Neeta to Rose. Her potion would wear off at any minute. I could feel her shake and cry.

I pulled the core group aside. We walked up to the barrier.

"Alright. Take our most advanced healers and spread them out. Two healers every thirty feet. You all know what to do." Neeta's invisibility faded. The girl was crying, her head facing away from the barrier.

I pulled Rose and Cilden aside. "I need the children to come through after me. And then you two. I want the others to see the children get through alive." The two were both hesitant but nodded their consent.

Kneeling down next to Rose, I put my hand on Neeta's head.

"Uncle Mike, I don't want to do it."

"It's okay, sweet girl. Remember when that nasty man made that mark on your arm?" She nodded, snot dripping from her nose. I wiped it away with my hand. "This is scarier than that. But it won't hurt as much. I promise. It's important that you don't yell, though. Can you do that for me? Can you be the brave little girl I know you are?"

She smiled at me and raised her fist up, still clutching the magic stone I gave her. I offered her a little fist-bump, a gesture I taught her months ago.

"Excellent. Now I'm going to go through first just to show you there's nothing to be afraid of."

I pulled up my character screen for good measure.

Secret name: Slanaitheoir (savior)

Character name: Michael Dian-Cecht
Race: Spirit Elf
Age: 27
Class: Undefined
Talent: Undefined
Level 8 (314xp to next level)
Health: 260 (180)
Mana: 355 (180)
Stamina: 180
Fatigue: 35%
Armor: 80 (1.1% damage mitigation) - 2.1% damage mitigation with
*   skills.*
Strength: 12
Intelligence: 16
Wisdom: 15
Constitution: 16
Agility: 12
Luck: 6
Alignment: Chaotic Good (+1)
Racial Traits: +5% to herbalism, +5% to all non-metal crafting, +5%
*   to nature-based healing and damage spells, +5% to mana*
*   regeneration*
Profession: Undefined
Company: Undefined
Modifiers: +20% movement speed, Spirit Elf (+10% to all damage and
*   healing done. -10% to all magical damage taken. +10% increase to*
*   all physical damage taken), 25% threat reduction, +8% to damage*
*   and spells (gear)*

I did some quick math in my head. The brand dealt 117 damage. With my new gear and my level increase, I would make it through the barrier with 26 health remaining. I wasn't comfortable with so little health remaining. I pulled out a healing potion and became ready to cast a healing spell on myself. I turned to Clifford and kissed him on the lips. Some of the others "awwed" at my loving gesture. He blushed a little. That didn't stop him from kissing me back.

"See you on the other side," I said. Chugging down the healing potion and casting living seed on myself, I felt the first few ticks of healing power course through my veins. I took two steps forward, spun to the left and pressed my body through the barrier. When the brand and the dark shell connected, a jolt of purple electricity spread over my body.

You are afflicted with 'Slaver's Retribution.' You will receive 7 damage every second for 30 seconds. After 30 seconds, the spell will explode and deal 24 damage. This cannot be dispelled.

I buckled to my knees, losing all sense of myself. Clifford caught me before I collapsed to the ground and helped me up. Despite wanting to scream with every fiber of my being, I held it in. I clutched Clifford's torso and held on for dear life, my muscles seizing as the dark energy coursed through my body. The final punch of the curse almost knocked me out. When my vision cleared, I was outside of the barrier. The mark on my shoulder had ruptured. A trail of hot blood was running freely down my arm. Only the scar remained. It took me another thirty seconds to reconstitute myself. I didn't bother healing myself to full health. I needed the mana for the others.

I couldn't stop blinking—an after-effect of the curse. In the corner of my eye, I saw that I had 116 health remaining. For the first time in what felt like forever, I saw the moon. The purple haze of the barrier gave way to a beautiful and brilliant twilight. I was mesmerized for a moment until Clifford pulled my gaze to him. I looked into his eyes, still dizzy from the barrier's curse.

"Can I do that again? That was wild!"

"Sometimes, I don't know what I'm going to do with you. You're a glutton for punishment. Now, Chief, let's get moving."

He called me "Chief." I liked that title. I didn't love being in charge, but I liked people trusting me enough to let me lead them.

I jumped back through the barrier to show the others our plan had worked. When they saw me moving back and forth, they began lining up in front of healers. I walked up to Rose to take Neeta from her.

"Not on my life, Michael. We're going through together."

I didn't fight her on this. She was the girl's mother after all.

"Okay, Neeta," I said. "Before we go through, I need you to drink this." I handed her a healing potion. "Then I need you to exhale as much as you can. Can you do that?"

Neeta chugged the potion down her throat without warning, Once swallowed, she exhaled. I activated the enchant on my ring. A bubble of protective magic encompassed her. Knowing it would last 30 seconds, I also cast living seed on her. Rose did the same to herself, and both of them stepped through the barrier, Clifford and I supporting them in the process.

Words couldn't explain how proud I was of the little girl. She handled the barrier better than me and, thanks to her plethora of rings, came out of it with more health than I had. She hung onto her mother, silently crying. "Did I do well, Uncle Mike? Are the guards going to come and take us away?"

"No, Neeta. You did fine. Better than fine. Look at Moga over there." I pointed at him. He had passed through the barrier and was writhing in agony on the ground until he blacked out. I analyzed him, thinking he had died. While dangerously low on health he did manage to survive.

"You have my permission to tell everyone that you're tougher than Uncle Moga, honey. Especially him. Never stop telling him that."

The girl began to giggle while Rose and I alternated casting healing spells on her to bring her back to full health.

With Neeta now taken care of, the rest of the plan went off without a hitch. Rose and I took turns pulling Junta and Cilden across the barrier, both using another charge of my protection ring. Once our friends were all safe, we worked on the queue of eager slaves still trapped in Elatha. Half way through the effort, both Rose and I had to take a break. Our mana was exhausted, and we were both dizzy and fatigued. We shoved some cakes in our mouth and swallowed them down with water.

"Why didn't I think to make mana potions?" I asked Rose.

"What would be the fun in that?"

"Did you just make a joke?"

"Yeah, but not as big a joke as when your mother made you."

Clifford and Cilden were both laughing at us, not sure how I managed to break so far into Rose's matronly shield to trigger her funny bone. I liked this new Rose. She was certainly the one person I would call my best friend.

It took an hour to get the hundreds of slaves through the evil shield. Some blacked out in the process. No one died. With most completely recovered, we walked down the hillside into the valley below. For the first time in four months, my map began updating again with new discoveries and information. Baridorne was carrying Moga over his shoulder, the little guy still out from pain despite the fact that we'd healed him to full health.

I took the opportunity to review my notifications. They offered nothing of note. I had increased my rank in Nature's Grace to 4, my rank in Living Seed to 18, and my Leadership skill to 12.

Once at the far end of the valley, a terrifying light shot across the entire sky followed by a shockwave. Magnificent, magical tentacles illuminated the sky above the treeline. They rose up above the dome encompassing Elatha, causing the barrier to look like a giant, celestial octopus. The arms fell under their weight and crashed into the dome. The sky illuminated with the light of a thousand lightning strikes. Those of us who were awake fell to the ground. The energy of the spell's shockwave would not let us stand.

When the light faded and our vision returned to normal, we checked the barrier a second time. It was still there, only thicker, darker, and more ominous.

"That would be the spell finishing," Nila said to me. "We haven't much time. In a matter of minutes, the alarm bells will ring. We stole over a hundred slaves from unsuspecting masters."

Nila and Clifford led us to a clearing in the woods. A giant stone platform occupied half of the glade. Both of them got to work, drawing chalk from their inventories. They etched strange symbols into the ground. It took them five minutes to perfect their design.

Clifford beckoned me over.

"I didn't tell you about this part because... I forgot." He wore a devilish smile. "We need your mana. Not just yours, mind you. We need everyone's mana for the portal to work."

"Why everyone's? I've seen portals before. They don't take much mana to open."

Nila had walked over to join us. She rubbed her chalky hands on her robes. "Normally, my mana would be enough for a small group of us. We're moving hundreds of people. The portal needs to stay open the entire time."

I nodded, turning my attention to the crowd. Everyone was awake now, eagerly waiting for me to make my next move. Panic began to set in when alarm bells signaled our absence.

I paused for a few moments to gather my words.

"You hear that? Those bells are the voices of our greedy masters. They want us back. They want you back." I pointed at an older woman. "They want your children back. And your grandchildren. They will never stop wanting to own you. You make their lives easy."

I pulled Nila and Clifford to my side. Someone screamed out "Kill the masters!"

"No!" I roared at the man. "Not all of them! Never all of them. These two here and the other masters with us today are not greedy. They've forsaken everything they know to set you free. They've abandoned house and home. They've exiled themselves from their families. Like us, they are now marked for servitude or death. Our fates are now intertwined. If we fall, they fall. If we live, they live."

Some began to cheer, but I quickly silenced them.

"And this one, Nila, needs you now. She has a small request. She needs our mana to open the portal that will take us away from this evil place. Will you give her your mana?"

Some shouted out "We will!" Others yelled out "We trust you, Michael!"

When the crowd was done providing consent, I instructed them all to sit down. Some were weary. The alarm bells from Elatha haunted them. They wanted to flee.

Clifford and I also sat down. Nila fixed herself in the center of the stone circle and began casting the most complicated magical spell I had ever seen. It was more like a dance than a spell. Her staff twisted in the air like a Hawaiian fire dancer spins his torch.

A gentle, white light drained from everyone in the crowd. Their mana was being drained from them. When mine started being drawn from my body, it was somehow different. My mana wasn't pure white. It was a stream of colors. Spheres of purple, blue, green, yellow, red, and blue swarmed around the center of my chest. They formed themselves into threads that tugged at my very soul.

Mana: 323/355

The filaments of my mana connected with Nila's staff, drawn to the call to amplify her spell. In the process, they pulled me along with them. I was pulled to my feet. And then into the air, strings of rainbow-colored mana abandoning my arms, my chest, my legs, and my feet. The crowd was awestruck. Some shuffled away from me, not sure what to make of what was happening.

Mana: 247/355

Nila saw me out of the corner of her eye, but couldn't stop now. She was too far into the spell. If she had stopped, it would have backlashed and could have killed her.

The filaments worked their way around my body, now escaping from a single point in my back. I was forced to spin around, arcs of magical energy being yanked from me now against my will.

Mana: 194/355

My mana pool continued to drain from me, illuminating the clearing in rainbow colored lights. It looked like 2 AM at a dance club. The waves of mana had formed themselves into translucent wings, now beating with the wind, lifting me further and further. Clifford was holding onto my leg for dear life, my steadfast lover anchoring me to the ground. A look of fear and awe painted itself across his face.

Mana: 123/355

At this point, some elvish slaves in the crowd postulated before me, including Rose. They appeared to know more about what was happening than I did.

Mana: 39/355

When I thought the experience would end, my mana began reducing into negative numbers. Light began to explode from my ears, eyes, nose, and mouth. The new light joined with the wings, now encompassing my entire body.

Mana: -61/355

At last, I heard a crack. Nila had banged her staff into the ground, and her spell materialized. She exited the stone circle, and a portal began to open, one with me still anchored to it. It wasn't until my mana had reached -500 that the light subsided and separated from my body. I hung in the air for a moment and then collapsed to the ground. Clifford and Nila both caught me.

"What was that?" I had to choke out the words one at a time. All of the air had left my lungs.

"Now's not the time. The portal will last only twenty minutes."

I nodded at Nila, regaining my footing.

"Alright!" Clifford yelled at the crowd. "Everyone up. Let's go. Our new home is waiting!"

The crowd didn't have to be told twice. My light show extravaganza was enough to reveal our location. I heard rumbles and roars of a mustering army heading in our direction. The crowd rushed to the portal like eager shoppers on Black Friday. Anything that didn't involve here and now was the best bargain ever. I tried to count them as they rushed by, concluding that there were nearly 400 here.

With the last of our new friends through the portal and only five minutes remaining, a line of soldiers stepped out of the tree-line. They were armed to the teeth, awaiting the order to attack, capture, or kill.

I was mesmerized by the attacking force, losing all focus on the task at hand. Only Clifford, Nila and I remained. The soldiers had begun to charge towards us. A wave of infantry rushed across the field. Clifford wrapped his arm around my torso and swept me off my feet. We jumped into the portal with arrows zooming by our ears. I cast my last two protective barrier charges on him and Nila. I tried to cast a healing spell on myself but was unable to draw any mana. One arrow hit its mark, sinking deep into my thigh.

In mere moments, the three of us were expelled from the portal, landing on rough ground. I rolled a few times, each spin pushing the arrow further into me. It didn't hurt that much. The bolt felt more like an ice cube on my flesh, adrenaline keeping the pain at bay. I pushed myself to my feet, coughing in shock, blood running down my thigh. My leg was nearly useless. The portal was still open with a line of soldiers running into it. My friends pulled me back and raised their weapons, prepared to meet whatever passed through the portal to our new home.

I had begun to lose hope when the window to Elatha narrowed. Some soldiers jumped out of the portal as it slammed shut. Only two made it. And an arm. And a few legs. I winced, feeling sorry for the soldiers who lost their limbs. The standing men, clad in the regalia of the Wraithheart company, spun around in absolute disbelief. After they had failed at finding their comrades, they dropped their shields and swords, held their hands up in the air and cried "We surrender! We surrender!"

It was at that moment that the adrenaline of our escape abandoned me. Pain overwhelmed me. I had a bleed effect. My health was low. I collapsed to my knees only to be caught by Baridorne. He suspended me in the air like a child clutching a rag doll, calling for the others to offer their healing aid.

15

"**E**nough already! I'm not a pincushion!"

The last hour was a painful one. When the portal slammed shut, and the imminent threat of death had ended, the crowd settled into a state of shock and disbelief. Some of them broke down crying, having been slaves for most of their lives. Those who weren't crying were celebrating their newfound freedom. A few were crowding around, watching me instruct them on how to patch a wound properly. Not that I knew how, although I'd seen enough fantasy shows to know that an arrow had to be pushed through, not yanked out. At least not without the immediate relief of healing spells.

My mana was still in the negatives and was regenerating slowly. Snails moved faster. In the last few hours, it had increased from -500 to -470. The consequence of my negative mana state was that healing spells didn't work on me. Nila tried to explain that healing magic worked in concert with a creature's mana. Her lecture was lost on me. I'd never seen negative mana before.

"So I'm technically not a creature?" I joked, words escaping from my seething teeth, holding onto Cilden while his wife tended to my wound. I was using every ounce of my remaining energy to avoid screaming in agony, a needle and thread tugging at my skin.

Rose had finished stitching my wound. She jumped for joy when I asked her to knit me closed. She had to tear my pants open while doing it, allowing cold air to caress every part of my nether-regions.

"Honestly. What do you people do when no one is around to heal you?" I asked the group.

"We die," Moga muttered, brooding and smug as ever. "Can we go now? I mean this is an excellent place to be and all. Aside from being on top of a cliff."

He was right. We had landed in the most inconvenient place possible. Now that I wasn't going to bleed to death, I had my first chance to survey our surroundings. The moon was nearly full, painting the entire area in silver. It reminded me of the spirit world. We were standing on a large plateau that met a sheer cliff face. The drop melted into a forest so large it extended to the horizon. I couldn't see a single light or fire within viewing distance. This place was very remote.

I pulled up my map and discovered that we were a few days south of where I first resurrected. To our east, a switchback meandered down into a broad valley. The moon didn't illuminate the valley. It looked more like a pit of darkness. The opening at the far end of the valley revealed a sea of silver, the open ocean.

Congratulations! You have found 'Brackenvale.' +40xp

"Where are the ruins?" I asked Clifford. "You said we would have ruins." I hobbled across the plateau in front of us, launching myself toward Petey. I was in desperate need of a crutch, and he was the perfect height. The young Trisian almost collapsed under the force of me but seemed pleased that I would use him for assistance.

Clifford joined me on my other side, pointing down into the vale. "It'll take us a few hours to get there."

"Wonderful. Let's get moving." My friends fanned out around me to begin directing the crowd. "Oh, and before I forget, let's bring them." I pointed at the two Wraithheart guards who managed to escape with us through the portal. "Can't be having them run off now, can we?"

"Are you okay?" Clifford asked me. "You're a bit manic."

I offered him a reassuring smile and took some deep breaths to calm myself down.

"I'm not okay. I don't know what happened back there. I intend to find out but now isn't the time. Let's get our people to safety first, okay?"

He rubbed the nape of my neck, offering both his compassion and understanding.

Turning away from me, he began to shepherd the crowd.

"You heard the man! Let's get moving."

We had to scramble down a switchback, stones crumbling under our feet. The walk wasn't dangerous. It was frustrating. Every time I thought I had solid footing, I slipped only to have Clifford and Petey catch me.

"How did you find this place?" I asked my companion.

"I didn't. My mother did." It was the first time he'd ever spoken about his mother. "She never told me how she knew about it. She made me promise never to tell my father. It was our hideaway."

As we walked further and further into the valley, rock face gave way to the forest. Colossal trees grew out of a blanket of thick, course ferns. The crowd had stopped. The path was overrun with the plants. Someone ahead of us tried to push the ferns away, only to pull back after being stung by them. He clutched his arm in pain, blisters forming from his fingers to his elbow. A healer had already started attending him.

Clifford passed me off to Petey like I was the object in a game of hot-potato. The teenager labored under my weight. Clifford walked towards the wall of ferns. They responded to his presence, lashing out and rustling around, compelled by some powerful spell to attack.

Raising his hands to the impenetrable wall, he muttered words of power inaudible to me. A rush of wind poured into the valley. The plants shook and trembled in its wake. In a single wave, the ferns retreated, curling and withdrawing until all that remained was a blanket of fiddleheads. The valley was now open to us.

"Are you going to tell me how you did that?" I asked

"Maybe when you get better."

Clifford took over now. Petey was exhausted, becoming more a problem than a solution. Clifford kissed me on my forehead, holding me up as our people filed by us. "Our people." That thought filled me with comfort and joy. It was good to have a community again.

They were all eager to find their new home. Many of the elves had bowed to me as they passed, whispering an unknown prayer under their breath.

Following the mass of bodies ahead of us, we continued into the forest. Even if the moon were shining into the Vale, the canopy would have hidden it from us. Instead, the moisture in the air offered its own illumination. The mist's glow was soft and warm, inviting me to fall asleep.

As we trekked through the valley, the moon had positioned itself overhead. Silver beams of moonlight cut through the mist to reveal a sea of sleeping fronds.

"Is this you? Is the fog a spell you summoned to put the forest to sleep?"

Clifford nodded. He was very pleased with himself.

"It only lasts another ten minutes. Enjoy it. We'll be to the ruins before then."

And he was correct. Five minutes had passed, and the tree line abruptly ended. The mass of bodies had already fanned out into a clearing ahead. We had reached the center of the valley.

The scent of moss and wood faded, replaced by the crisp aroma of dirt. The trickling sound of water pierced the air. Crashing waves echoed in the distance. The area itself was perfect, almost tailored to support a group our size. To the north and south, towering cliffs offered secrecy and respite, as though we were babies asleep in a gigantic cradle. The north side of the field was flat and damp, moon grass covering the entire area. A river skirted the area, one bank taunting the cliff above it. To the south, we found our trophy: a modest keep hugging the cliff. A large wall encased it, wide enough for foot patrols.

Congratulations! You have found 'Brackenvale Keep.' +40xp

I pushed Clifford away from me and hobbled forward on my mangled leg. I scanned the fort. I looked back at him. I studied the fort a second time. I looked back at him again.

"You. You just happened 'to have an idea' about where we could go?" I recalled his own words in his study a few months ago.

He shrugged. "It's alright."

I waved my fist at him in faux anger, pleased with the size and quality of the keep.

Over his shoulder, the forest behind him transformed. The haze had vanished, and the song had silenced. What was before an open wood with meandering paths was now a sea of stinging ferns ready to inflict pain and death on anyone who should mess with them. I was relieved at not hearing anyone scream in agony. We hadn't missed anyone when walking through the woods.

I wasn't mad at my companion. I was thrilled. And a little skeptical. I know that he came here as a child, but that was many years ago. While the forest appeared impenetrable, we had managed to get through. Others could have as well, either from the east by boat or the west on foot.

Our new settlers waited outside of the main gate. Exhaustion and fatigue overwhelmed them. Some had settled on the hillside, prepared to fall asleep at any second. I skipped through the crowd with Clifford as my crutch, catching up to Moga and Baridorne. The two were pressing their bodies into the stone gates isolating the keep. I almost laughed at the sight of my little friend. His face was as red as a tomato in July either from strain or anger. It was too hard to tell.

"Clifford, is it safe?" Nila asked him, waiting patiently by the front gates. The bags under her eyes looked more like a mask. I hadn't realized how strained the woman was by casting the portal. Hours later and she still looked exhausted.

"It is a ruin. No ruins are safe. The danger is contained, though. My mother and I saw to that years ago."

"What do you mean?"

"There's a rune on the gate that she placed there. If more than an animal got over the walls, the rune would be broken." He put his hand on the stone gate and muttered something. It wasn't a spell. His mana hadn't reduced. The large doors were repelled by his touch and screeched open revealing the village within.

"And there's a dungeon here. It hasn't been cleared in years giving the enemies within time to strengthen. Even my mother hasn't cleared the entire thing, and she was level 50."

"And the creatures can't leave the dungeon?" I finally joined the conversation.

"No. Just like Nott's Sanctum, they're tied to the dungeon itself. If they leave, they can die. That is usually enough to compel the creatures to stay put."

Pleased with his answer, we moved into the keep. With our weapons drawn we cleared each building. There were dozens of stone houses and a central manor the size of Clifford's Elathian estate. This building, however, was constructed into the cliff. More precisely, it seemed like the cliff had grown around it.

In clearing the homes, all we managed to find was a family of red foxes. They growled and screamed when we drove them away.

"Where's this dungeon?" I asked.

"Near the far wall." He gestured into the distance. "You should warn others not to go in there."

Our tour of the village was finally complete. My friends stood on the stone steps leading into the manor, eager to settle in for the night. The crowd of four-hundred freed slaves and former masters encompassed us. They had blank expressions painted on their faces. Most of them had spent their entire lives following orders. They were looking at the group of us, waiting for instructions from their leaders; waiting for instructions from me.

"What do we do now?" I turned to my friends with baited breathe.

"We do this." Clifford grabbed my hand and pressed our palms into the door of the manor. A notification's white text flashed in his eyes. He didn't consider it for long, and it quickly faded. A wall of text then filled my field of vision.

Congratulations! You have been transferred ownership of your first settlement! Brackenvale Keep. Current level 8.

This transfer is permanent. It cannot be rejected.

Congratulations! You are now the leader of your first settlement.
Transfer of ownership resets settlement level.

Name: Brackenvale Keep

Level: 1

Population: 417 (overpopulated)

Village Morale: Very low

Current renown: Unknown

Regional Defenses: Rocky shores, sheer cliff face, Acid Ferns,
Switchback, Hidden entrance to the valley.

Keep defenses: Ten-foot by three-foot wall, cliff face, gate and portcullis

Keep resources:

Water - Unlimited.

Food - Two months supply

Crops - None

Animal feed - None

Animals – None

Seed - One season

Weapons - Minimal

Notable buildings - Manor with war room, Stables with animal
paddocks.

Other buildings - 47 generic stone buildings. Allies: None Trade
Partners: None Enemies: Wraithheart Company

You now have access to this village's interface within the confines of
Brackenvale Valley.

You are now bonded to this village. Your resurrection location has been
fixed to here. This can be changed in one month.

Congratulations! You have completed the quest: "Let My People Go!"

This is an epic quest.

You have freed your friends along with 397 former slaves and 10
former masters. You have found them a new settlement.

Reward: +750xp, disposition gain with core allies.

Bonus Reward: +8,140xp (20xp per person), +1 moral gain for
medium-quality settlement.

Congratulations! You have reached level 9! You have 2 attribute points to assign.

Congratulations! You have reached level 10! You have 4 attribute points to assign.

Congratulations! You have reached level 11! You have 6 attribute points to assign.

Congratulations! You have reached level 12! You have 8 attribute points to assign.

Congratulations! You have reached level 13! You have 10 attribute points to assign.

Congratulations! You have reached level 14! You have 12 attribute points to assign. 1,791xp to next level.

Congratulations! Your disposition with Rose Thane has increased from Trusted to Ally! Congratulations! Your disposition with Junta Thane has increased from Friendly to Trusted!

Congratulations! Your disposition with Neeta Thane has capped at Trusted! Children cannot become allies.

Congratulations! Your disposition with Baridorne has increased from Trusted To Ally!

Congratulations! Your disposition with Moga has increased from Neutral to Friendly!

Congratulations! Your disposition with Peadair Byrne has increased from Friendly to Trusted!

Congratulations! Your disposition with Nila Hislop has increased from Indifferent to Friendly!

Congratulations! Your settlement morale has increased from Very Low to Low.

Attention: You are now known in the region as the leader of Brackenvale Keep. Your settlement renown is Unknown. Increasing your renown comes with rewards and consequences. Current Renown Reward: +15 leadership

Congratulations! Your rank in Leadership has increased from 12 to 25.

Congratulations! Rank 25 offers you the ability to form war parties. You may now command twenty-four other members in a single war party!

Congratulations! Your rank in Leadership has increased from 25 to 27

Clifford yanked my hand away from the door, and the notifications vanished. The crowd was silent, shock and awe written on their faces. I'd never seen so many open mouths in my life. I was also in shock, trying to process what had just happened.

My eyelids were out of control, unable to shake the information they had just processed.

"You just gained six levels in a few seconds."

"I did, didn't I?"

I took a moment to survey the crowd. I was their leader now. I had to take charge.

Walking down the stairs, I zoomed into the first person I saw that I hadn't met.

"What's your name?" I asked her.

The woman shook in my presence, unsure how to greet me.

"My Lord-"

"Michael, please. I am no lord here. I am your friend, and I hope you may one day be mine."

"Michael, I'm Clara." The woman pulled on her slave collar, a nervous tick many have adopted to cope with their lot in life.

"Clara, it's wonderful to meet you." I pulled the Trisian woman into a tight embrace, her rags scratching my chin. Releasing her, I spun her around to face the crowd.

"Everyone, I'd like you to meet Clara. She woke up this morning a slave of the Wraithheart Company. She is going to fall asleep tonight a free woman!"

The crowd erupted in cheers and applause. Roaring echoed throughout the village, bouncing off of the stone buildings and walls protecting us.

"Like you all, Clara is a woman of profound courage. Against all the odds, she rebelled against Elatha, a city cast in despair and darkness. She chose to live her life free from the chains of slavery and free from the malevolence of Ankou Levent and his master, Mannana." Some in the audience gasped when I said the High King's name.

"Now don't be like that. Whether you say his name or not, Levent will stop at nothing to see you back in chains. There's no power in his name. His power was in controlling us. And we took that from him. We chose to rebel. And we will continue to do so for as long as we are alive—and I have no doubt that we will be alive for a very, very long time."

Applause filled the square again.

"Now before I say goodnight to you all, I have two orders of business. One significant and the other common. When finished here, I need a group of you to organize and get water. You've each come from a specific household in Elatha. If there was a leader among you in that house, I need you to make sure everyone has food and drink before you go to bed. If you can't find food, come to the manor, and we will see you taken care of." Mumbling broke out in the crowd. They were all tired, hungry, and thirsty. Many expressed delight at seeing the day ending.

"My last statement for tonight, I promise." I could hear my friends behind me laughing.

"Tonight, none of us are members of or subjects to the Wraithheart Company. I am calling for the formation of a new company, specifically to govern and guarantee the survival and prosperity of our new home. Everything I have accomplished today is thanks to the grace and benevolence of a singular goddess. I was lost and alone. She became my source of light. I wish to dedicate our new home and our company to her. Like her, we will be the heart of light and healing for all the downtrodden of Vros. In every action, we will strive to purge darkness from this land! From this day forward, I name us 'Bracken Corps," named so after our new home.

The crowd erupted for a final time. Roars, whistles, and applause echoed throughout the valley. The elves in our company were all yelling something, bowing to me. The celebration lasted another minute before the crowd settled down and began filing out of the square.

Finally, only my closest friends remained: The Thatcher family, Moga, Baridorne, Petey, Clifford, and Nila. Standing in silence, we all considered one another with a sense of surprise and disbelief. We made it. We were now free.

The End

Secret name: Slanaitheoir (savior)

Character name: Michael Dian-Cecht

Race: Spirit Elf

Age: 27

Class: Undefined

Talent: Undefined

Level 14 (1,791xp to next level)

Health: 324 (244)

Mana: 419 (244)

Stamina: 244

Fatigue: 0%

Armor: 80 (1.1% damage mitigation) - 2.1% damage mitigation with skills.

Unassigned: 12

Strength: 12

Intelligence: 16

Wisdom: 15

Constitution: 16

Agility: 12

Luck: 6

Alignment: Chaotic Good (+1)

Racial Traits: +5% to herbalism, +5% to all non-metal crafting, +5% to nature-based healing and damage spells, +5% to mana regeneration

Profession: Undefined

Company: Bracken Corps

Modifiers: +20% movement speed, Spirit Elf (+10% to all damage and healing done. -10% to all magical damage taken. +10% increase to all physical damage taken), 25% threat reduction, +8% to damage and spells (gear)

Skills:

Novice Blades 1 (.25% increase damage): The ability to deal damage with knives and blades. Drains stamina. Increase in rank reduces stamina drain and increases additional damage.

Novice Staves 8 (1.8% increased damage, 2.5% increased chance to block). The ability to use a staff weapon to attack and block enemies.

Novice Grappling 1 (1% increase damage): The ability to deal physical damage through hand-to-hand combat.

Novice Light Armor 6(1% reduced damage/movement speed): Wearing light armor grants a bonus to damage reduction. Increase in rank improves movement speed and reduces damage taken.

Novice Observation 6: You are keenly aware of your surroundings. You are able to glean useful information from those around you to aid in your understanding of your world.

Novice Stalking 7 (1.6% chance of remaining hidden): The ability to stealth through the world. Increases fatigue. Increase in rank improves hiding, reduces fatigue increase and improves movement speed while moving silently.

Journeyman Herbalism (rank 45): The ability to craft powerful potions, elixirs, and poisons. Increase in rank to make mixtures requiring more ingredients. Increase in rank to make mixtures of better quality and class.

Novice Tailoring 1 (1% reduction in time to craft, quality of item): The craft of creating cloth armor and goods.

Novice Tracking 1 (10% chance to find trails and tracks in nature): The art of finding your way through nature. Useful for hunting creatures or humanoids alike. Also aids in discovering new paths.

Apprentice Leadership (rank 27): The ability to persuade and command others. Increase rank to be seen as a more effective leader.

Higher ranks provide skills unique to leading and commanding groups of people.

Novice Cooking (rank 5): The ability to create amazing items to reduce fatigue. Advanced creations offer other temporary benefits. Higher ranks improve quality of creations.

Spells:
Novice Nature's Grace I (rank 4): Cast this to infuse your target's wounds with natural magic, healing them for 3hp per second for 4 seconds. Mana cost: 10. Cast time: 1 second. This cannot be dispelled.

Apprentice Living Seed I (rank 18): Cast this to plant a seed of natural magic in your target to heal them for 4hp per second for 10 seconds. Upon expiration, the target is healed for another 10hp. Mana cost: 26. Cast time: 2.5s Increase the rank of this spell to increase its potency. Can be modified by Wisdom, enchantments, and racial abilities. Can be dispelled.

Novice Dual-Cast (rank 2): Weave two spells into one for 2.5x the normal mana rate. This may backfire causing damage and a waste of mana. Spells of the same type will be 3x more effective. Spells of varying types will yield different results. Chance of backlash: 50%

Novice Mana infusion (rank 3): Infuse your mana into a spell to amplify its effects. At your current rank, you must use all remaining mana. Increase in rank to gain more control over how much mana you expel.

Spirit Trek (no rank): Once per week, you may summon a portal to bring you and your party from your current location to your resurrection site.

Gear Equipped:

Staff of Druid's Healing. Quality: Exquisite. Class: Epic. Damage: 25-31 DPS. Can be broken by stronger weapons. Stats: +60 MP, +3% increase to healing and damage spells.

Tailored Scholar's Hooded-Shirt. Quality: Professional. Class: Uncommon. Armor: Light(5). +5MP. +20% to stealth when wearing the hood. Can be destroyed by weapons.

Nurturer's Leather Jerkin. Quality: Exquisite. Class: Rare. Armor: Light(20). Stats: +20 MP +20 HP, +2% increase to healing and damage spells. Set: 1 of 4

Nurturer's Leather Pants. Quality: Professional. Class: Rare. Armor: Light(15). Stats: +10 MP, +15HP, +2% increase to healing and damage spells. Set: 2 of 4

Nurturer's Leather boots. Quality: Exquisite. Class: Rare. Armor: Light(10). Stats: +20% movement speed, +10HP. Set: 3 of 4

Nurturer's Leather Bracers. Quality: Exquisite. Class: Rare. Armor: Light(10). Stats: +15 HP Set: 4 of 4

Mana-Dowsed Ring of Protection. Quality: Exquisite. Class: Epic. +35MP. Trigger to cast a protective barrier over a target that mitigates 25% of incoming damage for 30 seconds. Charges: 5/5. This item gains one charge per day until full.

Ring of Spell Storage. Quality: Exquisite. Class: Epic. Stores one spell for later use. This ring can only be filled once per day.

Ring of Lesser Magical Insight. Quality: Good. Class: Uncommon. +25mp.

Necklace of Healer's Might. Quality: Good. Class: Uncommon. Increases healing and damage of all spells by 1%.

ABOUT THE AUTHOR

RJ Castiglione lives in Rhode Island with his husband (and best friend). During the day, he works in software technical support. At night and on the weekend, he writes stories that he enjoys imagining.

Check out his website at https://rjcastiglione.com for more, including links to books two and three, Fjorgyn: The Deep Below and Fjorgyn: Shifting Sands.

facebook.com/rjcastiglione

twitter.com/rjcasta

amazon.com/author/rjcastiglione

goodreads.com/rjcastiglione

ONE LAST THING...

If you enjoyed this book or found it useful I'd be very grateful if you'd post a short review on Amazon. Your support really does make a difference and I read all the reviews personally so I can get your feedback and make this book even better.

And thank you to my friends over at The LitRPG Group and LitRPG Society for their support as well! We're all in this together.

Made in United States
Troutdale, OR
02/12/2024